D0053897

TECHNICOLOR PULP

TECHNICOLOR PULP

A NOVEL BY ARTY NELSON

A Time Warner Company

Warner Books, Inc., 1271 Avenue of the Americas, New York, NY 10020
A Time Warner Company

Printed in the United States of America
First Printing: March 1995
10 9 8 7 6 5 4 3 2 1

Library of Congress Cataloging-in-Publication Data

Nelson, Arty
Technicolor pulp / Arty Nelson.
p. cm.
ISBN 0-446-51819-0
1. Young men—United States—Sexual behavior—Fiction.
2. Americans—Europe—Fiction. I. Title.
PS3564.E4283T43 1995
813'.54—dc20 94-3338
CIP

Book design by L. McRee

To Hilary Beane

TECHNICOLOR PULP

PuIp1

26 and I'm at the end of the line again. Running scared down a dusk-soaked alley, the bricks whirl by me like black and red on a roulette wheel. I've run down this alley a thousand times thinking everyone is waiting to see my next move . . . Another cross-roads . . . I think it matters and it doesn't! None of it matters! It's all meaningless! Uh oh?! Who the fuck am I? An existentialist? . . . Look . . . I'm not some greasy european-looking guy, with a bob hair-cut, sitting in a cafe smoking hand-rolled cigarettes, plotting my own demise. I'm hiding. I'm running. I'm throwing up screens. I'm doing the dance. The Great American Novel's been squeezed through weak cheeks too many times. All I got is this story. A story of drifting. It's not my story. I'm just a small piece of it, sitting in Jack's apartment in Boston, lis-tening to the old man's voice over the phone. It's an old building with dirty stones, all pretty, and ivy

spilling off the roof. The windows are tall and skinny with chipped white sills cutting the sun off into a thousand glances. From inside, the windows look out over the city, down south of the building. Cars scream and honk off in the distance. Children laugh and play, and I hear the voice. I'm sitting on a green vinyl couch with one ear on the phone, one finger in my nose, and my head in China. Every once in a while, the voice raises in pitch and cuts off sharply, it's my turn.

"So yeah, anyways, um leavin' tomorrow, Pops."

"I guess it sounds great, Son . . . I'd like to go with you but I have to stay and work," he says with a fatherly mix of envy and sarcasm. I cringe slightly and wish I smoked cigarettes.

"Maybe I'll find some work over there, Pop . . . I don't know. I gotta chance to go to Europe and I gotta take it."

"Well, do you know anyone who might be able to help you get a job?"

Details! Details! The BASTARD always wants details!

"Doobe said he might know some people, but I gotta get there first . . . You can't set this kind of stuff up until you get there."

"You know more about these things than I do. I hope for your sake it works out," he pauses. "How are things with that girl you were going out with . . . What's her name again?"

"Lindsey."

"Yeah, how is she?"

"Things aren't too good actually, Pops. As a matter of fact, they suck."

"Well . . . You're both pretty young, maybe things'll turn around."

"Pop . . . If there's one thing um sure of right now, it's that things won't turn around with Lindsey."

The truth is that Lindsey's lost all desire to even touch me, let alone love me. Things are bleak. I can't really blame her. I've become a drunken pig and I don't think I'm fucking all that well anymore, either. I'm fat, bloated, angry, I don't have a job, and those are the obvious problems. I'd lose interest too, but . . . I'm the only interest I've got. I'm in love and I'm not in love. I'm free and I've never felt more trapped in my life. Good times are lean and these ARE the good times. Money is harder to find than a true blonde, and I can't tell the old man much of anything. I'm just trying to give him some vague suitable answers so we can both get a decent night's sleep. I adjust myself in my chair, arching slightly to stretch my back. I settle back in and yawn, studying the floor in front of me, glancing occasionally out the window at the children screaming. Even lying's become too much of a chore.

"Son, all I can do is wish you the best of luck. My life was different at your age," he pauses, "I didn't think about things the way you do. I became a lawyer because I didn't want to become a doctor and to tell you the truth, I don't know if the decisions

I've made in my OWN life were the right ones. At the time, I didn't feel like I HAD much of a choice."

Yeah, it's time now for my latest rendition of "My Great New Plan In Life" by Jimi Banks. Sung sweetly through the gold-plated pipes of yours truly to any number of fathers, mothers, brothers, sisters, aunts, uncles, friends, parents of friends, bartenders, godfathers . . . Whoever. Whoever's got the cash . . . Whoever's buying. Right now, I'm giving Dad a chorus of, "I know things look pretty stupid and aimless but it's all just part of that kookie, roundabout path to success I've chosen." If he claps, then I'll give him a little encore of, "It'll happen to me, just wait and see." It's all in the phrasing. I'm a regular Frank Sinatra of failure. All I need is a little dental work.

"Europe holds all the possibilities, Pops . . . And since I'm not there yet . . . It's tough for me to really go TOO into detail. I gotta good feeling about it though."

I don't wanna tell a complete and utter lie to the guy because, as long as we don't live on the same coast, we get along OK. You know, when I was younger I always wanted to tell the truth, but more and more, the truth got complicated and vague, if not downright UGLY. So much arguing over things that just don't change. I'm not ready to change and I don't feel like fighting about it. I have NO desire at all to be a rebel. I don't believe in anything enough to rebel against it. Who are these jerks that get all worked up and take over countries and start wars when they're, like, 23? I thought being young was all about having fun, and falling in love, and chasing dreams, and fucking. I don't wanna FIGHT about anything! I wanna FUCK! And anyways . . . I'm lazy. A busy day to me is three hours of phone calls to old friends, pleading for money to bail myself out of "some flukey jam that I just never even saw coming." When I was little, I wanted to be a pro hockey player when I grew up. Now I just like skating.

"I wanna find some hot duchess or something to take me under her wing and make me her pool boy."

"Sounds good to me, Son. Sounds better than what I'm doing."

The guy likes me, I think. I've really proven to him that I got the magic. He knows that life basically sucks. I'm like a cosmic soda jerk, serving up fantasy floats. Doing the things he only dreamed of as a youth. Beckoning to the child that romps deep in dad's soul. I have him back on the playground and I'm about to drive to the hoop for two . . . Or maybe five. We both need it. We both need to feel young again.

"So whatta ya think, Pops? I could really use a small loan to make this trip perfect. Maybe four or five hundred for that rainy day, or month, between jobs in London?"

There it is, so smooth, with that funny lead-in. I should be a pro. It's gonna happen, I think. Today's a good day. The pensive silence falls and my uni-brow moistens. . . .

"Son," he says, with restraint, "I never wanted to

have to say this to my own kid, but I'm starting to lose respect for you. I'm not going to tell you what to do with your life. I never have . . . But I don't want to finance it anymore, either."

Just like that. THE FALL. Jimi takes a deep blow that staggers him and sends him reeling. I recover, but only enough to retreat. I don't wanna throw any more jabs, not today. The father-and-son bout lasts a lifetime.

"Look, Pop, I'm OK. I got cash. A hundred bucks to be exact. Forget I said anything." Sugar Ray Robinson would've been proud of my backpedal, like a cagey deer.

We hem and haw for another two minutes and then it's over. LEAD BALLOONS. I hang up the phone. I've unconsciously popped up out of my seat and I'm circling around the room. I settle back down on the pea-green vinyl couch—the kind of couch that uses back sweat like superglue. I've been sleeping on it for three days. Every morning, I peel myself off it. It makes me feel loved. It makes me feel like the two-hundred-pound maladjusted decal that I am. The Cosmic Soda Jerk. The Dancer. I look out at the kids again. They're still yelping and running around free. Happy, and waiting for Bugs Bunny to come on. Getting chased by cute little girls, yelling and laughing through their chocolate ice cream beards. I could be like that. I'm just a couple hundred away. A wallet full of twenties and I'd be free again. . . .

Pulp2

"Hello?"

"Hi . . ." I stammer. "Lindsey?"

"Jimi!" she forces happily. "You finally made it off that rock of an island."

"Yeah, it was easy except that there was this baby on the bus in from the Cape that cried the entire trip. Two hours, straight through . . . Sounded like nipple deprivation."

She laughs. I hear her light a cigarette and exhale.

"So where are you now, baby?"

I hear "baby" and my head begins to convulse with delusions of amour. She loves me! Did you hear the way she said it! Life is beautiful. She loves me! She really does! I had it all wrong, maybe the old man was right! "Baby"! She said it with such meaning! I think I even heard her sigh!

"I'm at Jack's place in New Brighton . . . I don't think it's all that far from where you live?"

"Far? Baby, it's right up the street."

She said it again! Fuck London! I'm staying here with my girl!

"I know a great pasta place right around the corner from there—light veggie stuff—Why don't we meet there in two hours?"

"Lindsey, how do you know it's 'right around the corner'? I haven't even told you what street Jack lives on."

"Yes, you did, Jimi. You told me the other night when you called from the island . . . Remember that 'middle of the night profession of eternal love'? I'm the one who remembers all the highlights," she laughs, in control. Her voice always calm and soft, even when she's sad. Like she knows what she's doing on this planet, in this world. I feel like my own voice is always paranoid and sketchy, unless I'm telling a lie or having sex. Maybe that's just how I feel, how I reek, when I listen to myself.

"Jack's address was one of the 'highlights' of that phone call?"

"Well . . . Maybe not a 'highlight,' but I did remember it. Look, baby . . . I gotta run and make this study group for my Art History class . . . It's my major and I've barely looked at any of the material—postmodern stuff. It's really hard for me to remember any of it. Two hours . . . Don't get lost, and bring Jack. I can't wait to meet him . . . I'm gonna bring Lisa . . . You'll love her. See ya," and gives me the name of some nouvelle place down the street from Jack's.

"See ya" she says, all cute, and tells me to bring a friend. "See ya"! She's so comfortable with it all. She's so over it. So . . . Not what I am! I need passion. I need love. I need a good sweaty fuck to kill the pain, and she says, "See ya"! Her last words come down on me like a stone anvil, like a last chop to a rotting tree trunk. Bring friends, that dirty bitch! She knew just what to do. She knew I wanted to have a big *Gone with the Wind* scene and she killed it! I put down the phone. It's like some kind of masochistic tool. I'm some kind of masochistic tool! I'm dazed! I don't even want to go to Europe anymore! I'm only doing it to look cool to Lindsey! I could give a fuck about Europe! I don't even get a farewell Fuck and Cry session before I leave! I wanna carry the torch for this broad. I wanna cross the Atlantic with her picture taped to my boot! I wanna write her bad poems and wander the streets, starving, with only thoughts of her to nourish me! And she has to study for a fucking midterm! Doesn't she realize the gravity of this moment? Of our last night together before I begin my quest for Allah with a single bag of fish and chips under my arm?

Summer Love, what a BITCH come October . . . I sit across the table from her and I watch her. I watch her inhale and exhale her cigarette into a delicate plume of smoke. I watch her laugh and wish I'd told the joke. I watch her think while she listens to someone else speaking. Everything she does, every move, every sigh—captures me. I can't believe I ever went out with this girl, let alone lived with her. I study her from across the table, but she remains a stranger. She's all I thought I ever wanted in a woman. Seeing her for the first time, laughing, lighting a cigarette and tilting her head back, made me think that life's full of things we don't deserve . . . Gifts . . . Curses. I see her in my mind, walking down the street with her purse slung over her shoulder, in a hurry, simple, and beautiful. I always picture her from a distance.

I sit at dinner and I wanna leave. We're already just two people who used to know each other. I wanna cry and I want it all to be a memory, safe and sad. The sooner I get away from her, the sooner I can remember it MY way, instead of sitting across the table saying things like, "Could you please pass me the organically grown carrots . . . Thank you." I'm in a NEW AGE HELL and because I'm eating right, I'm gonna be in it forever.

Five Heinekens later, I'm standing outside the restaurant under a lamp, looking at her through the fog of my breath, wishing I had the guts to take my hands out of my pockets. Jack's waiting for me and Lisa's waiting for her.

"Yeah . . . So I'll give you a call from London . . . Or maybe I'll write you a letter . . . I'm glad we had a chance to get together before I left."

"Me too, Jimi, I'm REALLY glad. Wasn't that a GREAT dinner?" she says, as always too happily.

"Yeah, dinner was good."

"Lisa and I are going to the student union to get some notes for our test. I'm so happy. Lisa understands everything about all this modern art. I need THINGS in the pictures for me to remember them. Well, anyways . . . Call me," and gives me a hug and a quick kiss on the lips. "I'll miss you," and pulls away.

I stand and watch as she and Lisa walk down the street. Watching them talk and laugh, just looking at them. A kiss on the lips and an awkward friend hug and I watch as she gets smaller and smaller in the city night.

Jack and I walk and I'm too embarrassed to even look him in the eye. I'd raved so much about Lindsey and the chick had, at best, treated me like some geek she went to high school with. Friends from another time in life. A Time Past. And I guess we were because I felt that way too. It's crisp out, and both the city and Jack are quiet, too quiet, giving me time to think, which I just don't want. All the wrong turns, every bad joke and forced fuck run laps around my head. I blew it. It was me. Everything is my fault!

"So whatta ya wanna do . . . Go have a beer?"

"I wanna forget about that CUNT!"

"Cunt . . . I thought you liked her?"

"Jack, she devastated me and that's all I know! I can't take it. We were in paradise and then things got fucked up, and now, I'm in HELL!"

"She seemed pretty happy to see you."

"Happy! I wanted to move to Boston, sell shoes and live with that bitch! Open up one of those complicated bank accounts with all kinds of long-term potential, grow a fuckin' moustache! Wear loafers! Call it a life!"

The whole time I'm screaming, Jack's kicking a can down the street. It's making me edgy, like the clang of a hammer, over and over again.

"Jack, it's over." CLANG! "We don't laugh!" CLANG! "We don't cry!" CLANG! "We don't touch!" CLANG! "We don't fuck!" CLANG! "Jack!" I scream. "We don't fuck anymore!"

"Well . . . Let's just go home then, I guess," he says, walking. "Look . . . It doesn't sound too good but at least you're not banging nails for your old man like I'm doing."

I'm bleeding through the heart and this guy's giving me a Look At The Bright Side lecture. I'm supposed to be happy that I don't work for my dad, even though I just said good-bye to the girl of my dreams. Fuck work! Work is for people who can't lie! And I can't even LIVE in the same town as my dad, let alone WORK for him.

"You're right, Jack . . . Let's just go home . . . I'm kinda tired and I gotta get some sleep. It's my last night on the green vinyl couch. I feel like we've become close."

Jack and I'd gone to college together—hockey recruits. He blew out his knee and I fell in love with a bottle of bourbon. Real bonding stuff, watching our careers never happen together. Jack went to New Zealand after college, but he ran out of money, and now he's home building houses with his father. The guy's got heart. His downfall's his hair. The guy always has bad hair, ever since I've known him, and that's never a good thing to have.

"What time does your plane leave?"

"Six A.M."

"We'll have to leave at five."

"I'll probably still be up, thinking about how easy life was in junior high. The only thing that mattered back then was the cut of my Led Zeppelin T-shirt."

I'm laying with my back glued to the green vinyl couch, trying to peel an arm free so I can rest a hand on my crotch like . . . ALL MEN DO and I hear a phone ring two weeks earlier. I pick it up. It's Helms in London. He tells me to change my flight. I tell him that my current facade is collapsing at breakneck speed and I've got to get out of town as soon as possible. He tells me that Ray, our buddy, drove to a gorge outside of Aspen and hung himself. I meet Helms in New York and we go to the funeral. Oh, the danger that lurks in my head on a quiet night.

I lay restless, feeling the pain, and the freedom. A deep burning rages silently, until all that's left is charred and empty. When I feel that emptiness, it soothes me. Sweet peace whispers in the desolation. I see Ray, and I see Lindsey. I hear a song with Lindsey, lying naked on the beach under the sun. And then, life takes its course.

I have to go to Europe forever, I think. I can't be back in the States in two months, telling lies and losing jobs all over again. Growing up is bleak. More bills to dodge, less hair on my head, and GRAVITY. The world makes me old. I fight it, and that kills me.

. . . . I dream that I'm in the East Village, sitting in a crack shanty with a black guy named Champagne and two nameless strawberries—one on each side, rubbing my cock for hits of rock. It's the night of Ray's funeral and I've sworn off drugs but HERE I AM. I decide to grab the stash and run. The whole time I keep saying to myself, "Why did you just do this? I can't believe you did this?" I got no choice but to run once I've started . . . I run and I run . . . I run down streets and I run up alleys . . . I run around corners, through subways, and I see people I know everywhere . . . I wave to them all . . . Everytime I turn around, Champagne is right behind me with an angry mob, shouting and running faster and faster . . . Every dealer in New York is chasing me! I begin to tire and I start sinking into the ground with each step until I'm swimming waist-deep in concrete and the mob is on top of me. They're yelling, "Shoot the motherfucker! Shoot his ass!" And I'm sinking lower and lower, going, "I knew they were gonna shoot me. I fuckin' knew it! I'm such an idiot!" I can't believe I tried to run, completely trapped . . . A gun crackles . . . Not a TV gun boom, just a clean pop, and I feel a warmth in my back up at my right shoulder . . . The crowd stands over me, laughing and joking for a minute and then somebody puts a gun behind my right ear . . . I hear Champagne's voice. "Do it!" he screams and I feel a click . . . Just a click, and I'm on a roller coaster, plunging, screaming into a carnival of sirens and lights. . . .

Pulp 5

5 A.M. The streets of Boston asleep. It's quiet, quiet enough for me to ponder the magnitude of my journey. But I don't have the stomach for it just yet. I need at least two chocolate donuts before I can ponder anything deeper than the paste on the corners of my mouth. I just wanna snooze as much as possible before I get to London, so I'll have some juice for Last Call. I gotta fly down to New York first, and then catch a jumbo across to the UK.

The flight to New York is no big deal, just me and a bunch of commuters—corporate hotshots and their oriental counterparts, looking to swoop down on the Apple for a few gold-leafed worms. I'm hungry and all they have on the flight is some second-rate orange juice and some leftover peanuts. I want bacon and eggs. I want danish and plenty of it. I want pancakes with syrup, waffles drowning in fruit and I wanna go back to bed. Slight pangs of fear tickle the rim of my sphincter and I don't wanna think about it. I wanna think of it . . . As a simple itch. Christ . . . I got a hundred bucks in my pocket! I hope I don't find any bars I like or it'll be all over in a day! Doobe, friend that he is, told me not to worry, that everything'll be OK, that all I gotta do is get there, so I tighten my cheeks and squelch the fear as best I can. I still have a few tricks up my sleeve. And besides . . . It's too late.

We land at JFK and I find my way to the foreign departures section. It's about 8, and the crowd's beginning to buzz. New York's always good for a shot of chaos.

I find my gate and check in with the gay KEN DOLL-like flight attendant. The crowd at the gate fluctuates between the waiting line outside a bondage bar, and the extras set of Mary Poppins. Lots of leather and nose rings, sprinkled with a few tweedy british families walking around in order of height, like geese, like geese in plaid and wool. I settle in and a robot marches over the loudspeaker. It's gotta be a computer. I know things are bad but I can't believe any HUMAN could own a voice so monotone and soul-dead. Regardless of how long they've been on the pension plan.

"LADIES. AND. GENTLEMAN . . . FLIGHT. 7.8.1. TO. LONDON. AND. FRANKFURT. IS. ONE. HALF. OF. AN.

HOUR. BEHIND. SCHEDULE . . . PLEASE. DO. NOT. LEAVE. THE. GATE. AREA. . . ."

I don't even want to know why it's late. Each syllable karate-chops my skull. I look for a space on the floor to try'n catch a few winks. Last night's death dream got to me. I want to sleep but I'm afraid to. How many times can I die in my dreams and not at least wet my pants or drool all over my chest?

I haven't even LOOKED at a map of Europe yet. I haven't even READ one of those thought-provoking books like, "SO YOU'RE GOING TO LONDON." The truth is that I don't have much of a plan at all. I figure I'll get there, go to a bar, get drunk, and things'll work themselves out. That's what I do when I'm new in town. It always works, why won't it work in London? The less I know the better. I don't want some cheap preconceived notion about the whole thing. I've heard a lot about London, but I can't remember much of it. All the people I know who went there had money and I don't, so it's gonna be a DIFFERENT kind of town for me. I wanna forget about Lindsey and Ray or, I guess, DEAL with them, if that's possible. I'm paralyzed. The sadness is on me like a cheap brown leisure suit with big white stitch pockets. GRAND PICTURES. I got Grand Pictures. I remember it all bigger than it ever was. LEGENDS. MYTHS in my MIND. Lindsey's a Brigitte Bardot I actually fucked, and Ray is a John Belushi I actually got drunk with. SUPERSTARS in my small SAGA, and each died a tragic death—living or otherwise. Ray's dead but that's too real and I'm still too far away. Lindsey? . . . I can think about her. . . .

I see her in front of me with those big proud breasts and those round juicy hips, that dark hair falling off her smooth shoulders and that smile crying off her. Those breasts so proud, glowing like they each beat up Mike Tyson. I don't know where they get their power from or where this woman comes from—otherworldly. And I'm so THIS-worldly. The first time I saw her and that body, I made a sign of the cross. I felt it was TIME to start looking for a god, or at least, a shower with cold RELIGIOUS water. She made me smile, she made me throb. She was the only thing that ever stopped my running. I don't know what I run from . . . And I've never known where I was running to. All I know is that I never wanted to be WHERE I AM. The fat safe lie of school is over and nothing has worked out the way I planned. The world hasn't embraced me yet. Instead, I'm deep in debt and out of my mind most of the time. Bouncing around America, chasing Cassady's ghost and Kerouac's empties. A sad state of funny affairs. Thinking that life'll be groovy but finding taxes and insurance and people who've given up. Becoming one of those people, one of those lame fucks who sits around missing the Senior Prom. I was born, they stamped a nine-digit number on my forehead, my parents paid for a while and now . . . THE DEBT'S MINE! The best thing I can come up with is to run to the islands off Cape Cod and hide. Pretend I've found Heaven, but I haven't, not surrounded by a bunch of drunk fishermen with green teeth. All I've found is a decent place to wait it out. Then comes Lindsey and now, I'm back on my trusty Palomino of Fear, 28 minutes away from a new beginning and another ending. I got a car that's hidden from its true owner, the Repo-Man, behind a clump of trees. What do I do? Where do I go? New York's a big old tired concrete whore that lays waiting to be fucked, never giving a fair price to anyone. L.A.'s like a big TV that smiles and never believes itself—just a big inside joke. London's GOT to be the place. I'm lost in this country, too lost not to jump at a chance to get out. I'm on my way over to Europe where it all started for the whiteman. I need inspiration, stronger booze, a change of scene. I need a different world.

Pulp6

I'm laying down along a wall, next to some chick with platinum hair and a pierced tongue that wags its obscene self, every minute on the minute, across the lips and off the teeth. Pale skin wrapped in a black leather miniskirt and fishnets. Both ankles and wrists sport linked chain. I sit next to her feeling like a Peeping Tom in a woman's prison movie. On top, she's got a leather vest with nothing on underneath. Her breasts are of the extraordinary nature. How long does it take for a guy to get off the nipple, I wonder? She's reading an Anne Rice novel. She makes me horny. She makes me wonder what happened to my world that's got everyone dressing in homage to Bela Lugosi. As a rule, I don't like a woman unless she still has a hospital bracelet on. This starry-eyed dreamer has a gaze that harkens back to a world I DEFINITELY missed in all my reincarnations. She makes me feel normal. I'm so unintrigued by my OWN insanity. I just wanna lay next to her and purr. . . .

The next thing I know, I'm being kicked by a simple german girl with dreadlocks and nose ring.

"Ze blane . . ." she barks, "Zit's loadink!"

I jump up, still in a haze, and bound for the ramp. I finally fall asleep and the next thing I know I'm missing my ride. Dreaming about everyone I've ever known, swirling around in a big grey foggy toilet bowl. No big deal? I sit down on the plane and rub my eyes. Europe, no turning back and nothing to turn back to.

"Fuck it!" I yell loud enough to feel reckless. "I'm going." I let out a nice morning fart, eggy and wet, just in time to welcome a small bookish woman. Her hair shows signs of the swimming pool wars—green and straighter than Mother Teresa. I have a window seat with no seats in front of me. I'm in paradise. The blonde next to me could be an L.L. Bean poster child, and looks like she knows a thing or two . . . About everything. She also could use a few meals in her. Earthy widewales, a fishman's sweater, and not a single pouf of makeup on. Her hair is WAY straight. It reminds me of my college guidance counselor, the one who refused to talk to me after I dropped out one year. Yeah, suspiciously like that bitch! Probably read all those same OLDE english books that even english people don't understand. We say a quick uncomfortable hello and talk about the awkward smell on board. I look back out the window—one last glance at the States. I feel that feeling, that feeling of triumph from high school when my forged note from home would free me for another day. Nothing left to do but smile and run.

PULP 7

I open my eyes and I see her next to me, pale and shaking. Upright in bed with my fists clenched and throbbing, veins bulging in my forearms. My face buried in the blankness of the wall. Hyperventilating. I try to laugh for a lack of anything better to do.

"Morning," I gasp.

"Call it what you want to." She spits.

"Kind of a rough one last night," I add in subconscious defense.

"Yeah," she says, pointing to the mattress. I look down, knowing only too well but still hoping. No

Such Luck. Like a little boy . . . Pissed my bed again.

"Well . . . I guess it's better than blood."

"Well, if I'd known that was what you wanted I would've brought you into the bathroom with me ten minutes ago."

Waking up in a puddle of piss is old hat for us, more like an, "Ah Shucks" kind of thing. There's gotta be more to this story.

"Whatta ya mean, Babe?"

"I mean it isn't 'morning,' it's the afternoon and you've already made a DAY of it!"

The merry-go-round starts to wind slowly. The music grinding in my skull like a 33 playing on 45.

"I was in the bathroom a few minutes ago. I got my period a week early. That is . . . I guess it's my period. Forty-five minutes of you ripping into me and drooling brought it on early this month. I guess we don't have to worry about me being pregnant."

Some stories have no face, only images, flashes of color, and shards of sound—a merry-go-round, like I said before . . . Of Shame and Horror. Doing things I never thought I'd do . . . Things I can't remember.

"You came in . . . I was in watching TV . . . Do you remember coming home?"

"No," I say . . . But really I do . . . Just not that much of it . . . Just shadows, a laugh here and there . . . Pressure on my eyes . . . The sweat on my forehead . . . Some voices.

"You actually pulled my top down and started sucking on my boob in front of everyone in the living room . . . You kept saying that you thought it was SEXY . . . I knew you were beyond stopping . . . So I came in here with you."

The story begins to take horrific form . . . The shame tightening my lungs making it hard for me to get air . . . Spinning . . . I remember faces in the living room . . . A nipple in my mouth . . . A hand across my face . . . Pushing . . . Laughter . . . Arguing . . . Someone cheering . . . Someone throwing pillows at me . . . Me like an infant . . . Pushing with my face against a hand. . . .

"Your nose was bleeding . . . You smashed your face against a chair while you were crawling around on the ground . . . Then we came in here . . . And you shut down completely . . . You didn't even know who I was . . . You were disgusting . . . Blood and spit dripping off your chin . . . Telling me to rub my clit so we could be in love again . . . Asking me if I liked it . . . You're such a pig . . . Like I love being pounded into until I bleed . . . Asshole . . . I gotta get outta here . . . You said you'd change . . . But you can't . . . You've lost it!"

Listening to HER story . . . Hearing who I am, or what I can be . . . I remember the bottles . . . And the laughter . . . The sun . . . Coming home . . . People laughing at me . . . And the nipple in my mouth . . . People yelling at me . . . Not caring . . . Not caring what they think of me. . . .

"I just shut down . . . Asshole . . . I died . . . I let you fuck a corpse . . . All I could do to save myself . . . Was to die . . . It was all I could do . . . And I let you just rip into me until you finished . . . And then you passed out . . . I laid there next to you . . . And then you starting puking all over the place . . . Then you passed out again and pissed in the bed . . . You just mumbled through it all." She says, looking at me in utter disgust, "Look at yourself . . . JUST FUCKING LOOK AT YOURSELF!" And begins pounding on my chest. I cover my face and absorb the blows. Each hate-filled blow actually soothes me while my head begins to kick out pieces of the final minutes. The final moments that I remember in bed . . . Pounding . . . And grunting . . . Hoping that an orgasm will bring back our love . . . Just one more and she'll love me again . . . We'll be happy . . . I know we will . . . Rub . . . Yeah . . .That's it . . . Rub . . . Rub it and all of this will go away . . . You'll only remember the fun parts . . . Rub it long enough and you'll only remember the good parts . . . Gasping . . . Searching . . . Trying to find the love again . . . Her screams . . . And the fists on my chest . . . Every once in awhile catching me in the head . . . Until finally . . . She stops and begins to cry . . . I try to hug her . . . But she recoils . . . I feel the loathing in her limbs . . . It's beyond her . . . She is beyond me.

Pulp 8

We roll over top an endless blue shag. So calm, the ocean, a painting at 20,000 feet. Sharks rip tiny fish into finger foods and all I see is a huge blue pillow.

"No, thank you. I don't eat meat. I phoned the airlines in advance and I SHOULD be getting the vegetarian plate. I'll eat chicken, if I must, but DEFINITELY, NO RED MEAT."

It's the woman next to me. I knew it'd be a matter of seconds before she'd start ASSERTING herself.

"Hi, how ya doin'?"

"Hello . . . Fine," she scoffs.

"I couldn't help but just hear you and I was wondering, are you a devout vegetarian? I mean like izita philosophical thing with you? Or are you just healthy?"

"Actually, I WILL eat meat. I just PREFER vegetables, especially in London."

Very relaxed, no second-guessing words. I admire that in a woman . . . Scares the hell outta me.

"So, you've been to London before?"

"I've been studying in London for six years. I'm on my way back to complete my thesis on the Bronze Age. I've always been an Anglophile and

Archeology is my chosen field of study. It's been an excellent opportunity for me to fuse together two things that I treasure."

"I know what you mean. I always wished somebody'd make a movie where the Flinstones meet the Jetsons," I say, not quite sure what the Bronze Age is.

"So why are YOU going to London?" she says.

"It's kind of a long story but . . . Really, it amounts to a basic desire to see a friend and leave a few behind."

"Really," she hesitates, "I thought maybe you were in school."

"No, that nightmare is long over."

"You didn't like school, I gather."

"School didn't like ME and I REACTED to it. I weighed too much, in the eyes of my professors, to appear capable of grasping the ethereal qualities of the Classics."

"I see?" she says, with a fidget. I look at her hair outta the corner of my eye, greasily tucked behind her right ear, and spot a certain confusion in a fresh bloom of perspiration.

"School, to me, was more of a sixteen-year seminar in What I Don't Ever Want To Be—a preventative thing."

"I'm not quite sure I follow . . . The physical weight thing seems kind of odd to me."

"I gutted it out long enough to grab my sheepskin, wave it at the family, and run . . . I've spent the last couple of years going to great lengths to forget everything they taught me in school."

"Your experience sounds so . . ." she pauses, ". . . Unpleasant."

"It wasn't that bad . . . I read a few books I never woulda forced myself to read."

"The Classics?"

"Exactly."

"Any favorites?"

"*The Scarlet Letter* . . . I sometimes fantasize about Hester Prynne to this day." She gives me a subtle Marty Feldman look.

"My name is Karen by the way."

"Hi . . . My name's Jimi." Our introduction, more of a good-bye than a hello.

PULP 9

The minute steak and powdered eggs've made me drowsy. I put my seat back and turn off the overhead. My dream state takes me back out the window. It's dark outside and it feels good to be above the clouds. I drift along nursed by the hum of the engines. I see why my cat sleeps on my chest at night—a massage to the soul. I feel quiet . . . I'm not asleep . . . I'm in and out . . . I just don't feel like having my eyes open. . . .

"WE ARE APPROXIMATELY TWENTY MINUTES WEST OF LONDON'S HEATHROW AIRPORT. THE FLIGHT ATTENDANT WILL BE COMING AROUND WITH IMMIGRATION CARDS. IF YOU DO NOT HAVE A PEN, PLEASE RAISE YOUR HAND AND WE WILL GET YOU ONE AND . . . PLEASE . . . BE PATIENT."

It's gotta be half the problem with this lame world—too easy to travel. It used to be that if someone wanted to go somewhere, they really had to WANT to get there. Nowadays . . . It's a matter of making a phone call to the airlines and booking a flight. OK, so every once in awhile a plane drops out of the sky, BIG DEAL. I'm talkin' cannibals, or hurricanes, or deserts—things that slow down a trip. When's the last time some poor bastard got buried up to his neck by Apaches and slowly eaten by huge red ants? It just doesn't happen anymore! Traveling used to be a sign of vision and courage. Now it's all about leisure and cash.

I see the United Kingdom off to the left of the plane—a huge galaxy of islands, painted by a string of lights that shoot off in every direction and come back into a thousand circles. I'm landing on another planet. No grids? Every street with a mind of its own, roaming where it pleases—an elegant chaos that busts America for the capitalist graveyard that it is. Here pal, you work at E–23, and sleep on the south corner of L–97, and fuck your old lady at Z–49. When it's all over, your corpse will reside in T–65—It's a nice plot. So . . . Pre . . . De . . . Ter . . . Mined.

The stewardess passes out immigration cards. I've

never even heard of the things. I peek over Karen's shoulder and do whatever she does. I figure that she's a pro at this kind of thing—probably took a seminar on the shit. It's crystal clear to me now. No prior knowledge. I'm free. A worm reborn in another land. My only luggage—a muddy conscience and a few cool T-shirts. I didn't even remember to bring socks or underwear.

PULP 10

The plane touches down and everyone begins to panic in their seats. So terrified that they might be the last ones off the plane. So scared that someone might get in front of them, or just LOOK like they know MORE what they're doing. I have to hustle myself because I'm trying to follow Karen and she's moving down the aisle like a hooker in debt. I don't get it, nothing the chick studies has changed in a couple thousand years! How many archeological breakthroughs can there be on any given day? She's moving fast. I gotta elbow the simple german girl just so I don't crush this old lady in front of me wearing a flowerpot-like hat on her head. The hat blinds me for a second and I panic, thinking I've lost my way out. The airport's a blur. My eyes are glued to Karen as she navigates through the crowd.

She doesn't let up the pace until she hits customs. I'm not talking to Karen anymore. I'm simply using her to get from point A to point B.

The line I'm in is the longest. It reminds me of staggering home drunk, wishing every nextdoor is home. Waiting, with nothing to do but think of the rest of my life. Counter 22 opens up just as I'm about to buy my second house in the suburbs with kids who don't trust me and a wife who eats for all of us. There's a very normal-looking, middle-aged, bearded guy at the helm. He's sporting a sweater of brown and, as I soon find out, reeks of the most putrid tobacco—stale socks treated with cat piss and aged in a sauna. Nothing short of severe childhood trauma could make a man smoke tobacco that smells like he smells as I walk up to him. He takes one look at me: the pompadour, the burnt eyes, the fake Beatle boots, and I know there'll be questions. His moustache is quivering and stale sweat beads frame his face.

"So . . . Lad . . ." he says, ". . . 'Ow long do you think yu'll be in London?"

"I don't know . . . Maybe six months or something like that?"

"Quite a holiday? 'Ow much money do you have with you?"

He's baiting me. Trying to make me pay taxes. I know it! I'm pissed Helms never told me about this! I hate to NOT KNOW when I'm fucking myself up!

". . . About three hundred dollars."

"Three hundred dollars?" he snaps, all jolly and arrogant. "That isn't quite a lot of money now, is it?"

"No, but I think I'll probably get more from home when I get settled in."

All the other lines are moving along, as I sink deeper and deeper into the immigratory quicksand. What are they gonna do, make me go home for being broke?

Things go from bad to worse and within minutes, I'm in a small blank neon-scorched room with two very similar gents who are making it their business to know my business. I'd say from the way the one guy is cupping my ballsack, that the gang all got together and decided that I'm a smuggler. It's an offhanded compliment for any loser to be considered dangerous, and I stand proud as they gauge the weight of my testes and rifle through my journal. This goes on for ten minutes until they're satisfied that I'm just lost and not really a threat at all. They tell me, snickering, to have a nice stay in London and stamp my passport.

The violation of my person puts a bounce in my stride. A *Reader's Digest* version of *Midnight Express*, I think, and so like me to be overestimated. I shoot through the gates and eye up a row of tellys along the wall.

I don't know what happened to Karen. I imagine she made it through customs and is already off in the corner of some library, unearthing ancient trivia.The thought that I may never see someone again, even a total stranger, depresses me. I didn't really want to thank her, it's just that I'm afraid I only get to meet so many people in my life and I always wonder if I'll know when I reach the halfway mark. When I'm not contemplating suicide, I'm praying I'll never die. I need a lot of time to come up with a good idea, or at least, a rap that everyone thinks is cool. I need to see the world and I need to find home. I need to sleep with a million women and I need to find THE ONE, all while deciding whether or not I even like women. I wanna be a starving artiste and I wanna be a rich pig-man. I wanna be real and I wanna just sell out for the irony of it all. I wanna be the priest who marries Woody Allen and Axl Rose. I wanna be Madonna's flower girl when she finally marries . . . Herself.

PuIp11

Crafty me, with my Beatle boots and my Kool-Aid smile, realizes while standing in front of the telephones, that I don't even know what kind of cash the british use—something about "quid." My deliberate naivete is beginning to be a pain in the ass, already. Mister Open-Road can't even make a phone call. The Crisis of Everyday Life. The thud of concrete anxiety circling over me with its vulture wings, when an oasis appears before me in the shape of a currency exchange booth. I look up at the charts and know that money, in my life, is a dying, howling beast. My first of six twenties is snatched up in return for eleven pounds. I tell the nice lady that I need to make a phone call. She takes back a single pound and gives me smaller coins. I thank her and she says, "Cheers."

Each phone booth is a tiny hut, painted red with yellow trim. They invite me inside. A long ways from the grafitti-stained piss-reeking cubes back home. This world is not real to me. The sounds, the smells, all different. My pulse quickens, things to figure out. I call Doobe's number, after three rings a female voice says, "Hello?" and I ask for Doobe.

"He's on his way to get you," it says, without offering a name. I thank the voice and hang up. I find a warm corner and strike a pose—try to look pensive. I hate to wait.

Time passes, not much, and I see yellow bell-bottoms, a pillbox hat, a suede fringe vest, and big black bubble-top shoes—Helms. I'm happy to see the guy, walking feet out like a proud duck with arms swinging high above his head. Not loving Helms is like hating cartoons.

"Jimi!!!"

PuLp12

We jump on a train, Helms and I, sit down and start swilling on a pint of cheap scotch. My friends are my heroes, fuck Peter the Great.

"I don't know what I like more . . . This scotch, or those yellow bell-bottoms, Helms . . . They both remind me so much of how low I've sunk."

"It gets a lot worse, Jimi . . . You might remember this scotch like it's CHAMPAGNE some day."

The scotch is bad. I taste broken dreams in every sip. I can only hope it gets better as the night goes on—the saving grace of all shitty booze. The train does a strung-out hula down the track, forcing caution on every futile gulp. Everything happening to me is grounds to stop drinking, I think, as a missed shot rolls down my chin. I look at Helms with his silent-movie smile, feel good about my childhood and think logic is as useless as denial.

"Jimi, we ride this train for ten more minutes or so and then we gotta hurry to catch Last Call over by my place."

"Whattaya mean, Doober, 'Last Call' . . . It's early?"

"Last Call's at eleven o'clock."

The number "11" strikes me deaf with a dumb look on my face. I'm devastated. My european fantasy trip spills out of the gutter and into a suburban hell before my shocked eyes. What has life come to? What was I thinking and why didn't I ask such a vital question? More importantly . . . Why didn't Doobe warn me? My liver begins to sweat.

"Doober . . . What am I gonna do here? All I WANT to do is sit around brassy woody pubs and mooch drinks off newfound friends."

"I thought you knew . . . And anyways, what does't matter now?" he says with a slap to my insecure and manly cheek. "You might have to actually DO something here other than sit around and get fucked up," he chuckles.

"Helms, I LIKE to kill large chunks of time with a cool elixir in my hand. I have fun when I do that. If I wanted to go sight-seeing, I would've stayed home and looked at fucking books! I didn't come over here to get Zen-like, 11 o'clock, no wonder this fuckin' EMPIRE fell!"

PULP 13

So now I get to the part about being in London for the first time. London, to me, was always just a big collage of bad plays I saw on public TV growing up—Channel 13, I think. A lot of capes and top hats, and people being witty in ballrooms. MANNERS. Dickens and poor people. Little awnings on the houses. 200-year-old-looking signs on all the buildings. All that corny old nostalgic shit. Old men with rotting teeth and their women with the heavy bottoms.

We jump off the train, cut through the station and hit the neighborhood drag—a small strip of shops, taverns and steps, a lot of steps. It's quaint, visions of *Mister Rogers' Neighborhood.* Rows and rows of town houses with funny little cars parked outside of them—turn-of-the-century cutting-edge go-carts with windshield wipers. Street lamps, all glowy every which way, perfect landmarks for my blurry eyes. Every house has odd-shaped windows, all made to NO order.

"Jimi, there's a pub here for every different brand of ale. The breweries own the pubs."

"I fuckin' love it! Um gonna roam these streets like a human camera—my heart in one hand and my cock in the other. Nothin' but . . ."

"I'm not sure how the locals will feel about that camera stuff, but they'll appreciate your enthusiasm I'm sure. Let's just take a second here, Jimi, and relax before we go in the door."

We're outside a pub at the top of Doobe's street, which is now my street. Right in the center of town, there's a bus stop and benches and a little monument of a guy on a horse looking brave. I peek in the window. Even the pets hang together in the pub. Homey, all wood and brass, just like I thought. There's even a fireplace. A great place to spend a life, or a day, or maybe just the better part of my twenties.

"Perfect, Helms. I couldn't be happier. The whole fuckin' trip was worth it for this moment! Something in this world is just how I thought it would be!"

"Jimi . . . I'll do the ordering when we get inside," he says, with what really sublime and sophisticated writers would call HUSHED TONES.

"Helms, you don't understand, you Tom Cruise motherfucker with Dudley Moore hair and teeth! I love pubs! I'm not a club guy!"

"Easy boy, I know you do. Let's just save the THAT'S JUST WHO I AM speech scene for a little later on."

Maybe Helms is right, maybe the scotch's hit me harder than I realize, maybe a nice beer would be in order. I follow Doobe into the bar. We sit down, the pub's noisy and I get the feeling that it's almost over. The 11 o'clock thing is already fucking with my life.

"Doobe, maybe Spain is the answer . . . Maybe we gotta go to Spain and chase bulls with big glasses of rum in our hands?"

"Let's just celebrate your safe arrival, Jimi, cheers," and we ching mugs. I sit back and let the room-temp suds swish around in my stale mouth.

Families, laughing and drinking together, and I'm so far away from any kind of home. I hear all the children laughing, and it makes me think that I was once a child, that I am still a child . . . I need to get out of this rut . . . I need to get out of me . . . All the families, from Grandpa to the tiniest babes, and I don't want to do anything but sit or run, sit on a barstool or run away. I'm in a rut and I can't see it any other way . . . I only see the end . . . I'm blind to the beginning . . . I'm tired out when I need to be fresh . . . It all just started and I'm already looking back on it.

"It's good to see you, Jimi." I peer at Helms through the cool amber of his glass. He looks so pretty. The bartender is shooing us out the door, telling us to finish up. I see Helms and I see the children. I'm snapping pictures, sitting safe behind some lonely filter, prisoner in my own TV. What would Jim Carroll do? I am not anything . . . I'm a bloated potpourri of other men's actions . . . I don't do anything unless I think someone cool did it before me . . . I'm a follower trapped in a unique mouth . . . I've never done any of this. I look around. They want me to leave. I should leave. I see Helms, all safe, drowning in amber. A looking glass . . . I hide behind a looking glass . . . I'm a being, crucified on an antenna. Fuck You Jesus! I thought you did this for me! I thought you did this already! My blood is your blood. I thought my blood was your blood. Looking through the cool amber, all the voices once removed, talking to me, shooing me out the door. Telling me to leave, I'm hearing that I'm welcome.

PVLP 14

We order a pizza from across the street and roll home. The "flat" is really a two-story town house with no furniture. Naked lightbulbs dangle down, coloring each room. I meet Sonja and Loren. Donald, the last of the roomies, is off at "Mum's" in the country. They're playing cards, and we sit down. There's hash on a small tray—good black hash, and Helms lights a pipe. I'm on the floor. I take a drag, and the pizza arrives with a bottle of white wine. I twist off the cap, take a swig and hope for a sense of humor. Helms opens up the pie, which looks good except for one small but large detail. There's an egg in the middle of it. A beautiful big fat pizza, dripping with cheese and so much spinach, and there it is, smack dab in the middle—one close-but-no-cigar chicken!

"What the fuck is THIS thing?"

"It's an egg . . . Wha'does't look like from where you're sitting?"

"I mean . . . Yeah . . . It looks like a fucking egg, but what's it doin' in the middle of this pie?"

"Is this ANOTHER thing I should've warned you about, Jimi? . . . Well . . . I'll tell ya now. You're in London and they put eggs on a lot of things."

The girls are laughing, finding humor in my small-time dilemma. I look down at the egg, all yokey and drippy, polluting my cheese. The cheap scotch gurgles in my stomach. More hash, it'll take more hash before everything mixes up alright.

"You just toss that egg over my way when you run into it. I'll eat it."

"You'll eat anything, ya fuckin' vulture!"

"I don't like to waste food, Jimi."

"No, you're a pig! That's what it is! It's got nothing to do with waste!"

I bicker helplessly for another minute, taunted by the girls' laughter. I can't take it when girls laugh at me. I got no choice but to take a taste. Embryo on my nice pizza! Some things just shouldn't BE in some places.

The girls are playing gin rummy, and we join for a couple of games. I don't know how to play, so the game slows down. Doobe's trying to cheat and Sonja's all over him. Off the face-up pile, over and over again he tries, and she never misses it. I don't either but I don't care. Doobe always cheats. It's part of his game and I can respect that.

"Bloody Helms! Put it back in the pile! You're a damned cheat."

"I got it from the pile," he says, mouth agape, "you're all watching, what could I've done?"

"You could've done just what you bloody did! Which is cheat!"

Sonja's sharp, too sharp to be happy, and the hash doesn't slow her down a bit. I'm beginning to think I love her. Could she be the answer? Could her foreign loins be the launching pad of my tranquillity? Maybe I need an-other woman? Her bored look, her strong calves, hips lost back in the fifties, all Marilyn-ish. She could be the answer. I start to fantasize about a life with Sonja, my head wrapped in her cynical thighs. Every once in awhile my dream is interrupted by the missus catching Helms in the act of cheating once again. He always argues his case before he replaces the misdrawn card. And then, he's always good for one more shady move. I float over to Loren. Dark-skinned with teeth of pearl—what a combo. Sparkling pearls on a string running through cocoa skin and golden brown tresses. Hair pulled back to reveal a flawless face wrapped in a constant smile. What a pair of women I now live with! Sonja, blasé, knowing and indifferent, taught by life not to care, heart polluted by the sum total of her experience. Loren, laughing and smooth, nice enough to make me act like me. Didn't I just meet these girls? Is it the hash or am I seeing?

We play cards for about an hour, and then the girls go up to bed. Helms falls asleep watching the telly, which gives me a chance to sneak up to his room and make for the bed. I deserve it after my stint on the pea-green vinyl couch. I lay awake and think about my day. Being with Helms makes me think of Ray. I start to wonder what Ray thought about as he climbed to the top of that bottomless mountain pass in the Rockies to string himself up in a tree, waiting quietly to be found blue and lifeless and tragic the next day by people he called his friends in a note. Maybe I didn't even know Ray anymore by the time Ray ended. Maybe the guy I hung with was long gone. A lot can happen in a year or two. A person changes, and then, I don't know Ray anymore. I begin to think about the island, and then, of course, it's about Lindsey and I feel the adrenaline of self-hate burn through my veins. Feelings run through me, pouring out over my chest like hot piss on cuts. Victimized by my past, by my part, swimming in black, and anger, and frustration . . . I don't want to feel at all . . . I want to forget . . . Forget the lesion that bubbles in the back of my brain . . . A little tumor swirling inward . . . I go inward and I drown . . . Ray is dead and I'm left cursed. Should I be sorry? Was he sorry? Is it worth being sorry? I don't want to grow from any of this shit. I don't want to have to feel all this shit! Let me fall asleep! If you love me, let me fall asleep, Jesus, you motherfucker! Staring up at the ceiling, screaming in my head, needing something bigger than me, or Ray, or life, or any of this shit. All of this shit!

Pulp 15

Was I sleeping? Or was I hanging off the edge of a cliff for six hours? Either way, it's over and the sun is up. I shoulda gone jogging for the night. My teeth are stuck to my lips. My throat is raw and cracked like an abandoned concrete shoot. I die a thousand petty deaths at the start of every day. I remember part of a dream, something about standing in a McDonalds and it's windy and I keep trying to order a Big Mac but I don't want the Special Sauce. I just want ketchup, and the girl behind the counter keeps saying, "You, Jerk! We don't serve Big Macs with ketchup. It's Special Sauce or forget the whole thing!" She's laughing in my face but I won't take "NO" for an answer. It's a stalemate. Everybody's always laughing at me in my dreams and nobody ever tells me why. I hear a phone ringing in the back of the restaurant. My eyelids roll open and I see that the phone clearly IS ringing. I wait two more rings and then get up to try and answer it. I'm a good three steps away from the phone when I hear the final choke of its bell. I walk back upstairs. Doobe is stretched out on a piece of grey foam next to my nice box spring.

He opens a tired eye, spots me, and slams it shut in a sarcastic wink.

"Thanks for waking me up last night, James. Nice guy . . . That chair was real cozy at about 4:30 in the morning."

It's the old full name thing—a sure sign of some hurt feelings.

"Pal, it was so late . . . I barely even knew what I was doing and besides . . . To wake you up would've all but condemned me to a night on the floor . . . I just couldn't do it to myself."

"You gotta a big heart, Jimi . . . I'll give ya that, but I'm still waitin' for the day when you use it on somebody other than YOU."

"Doobe baby, when the day comes! When my ship comes in, I'm taking you to Rio for Carnivale . . . I know I owe you. Don't think I'm not keepin' track of all you've done for me."

"Um gonna pray that day never comes. Who knows what else will've happened by then," he says and jumps up off the floor. I catch a short right to the ribs and he's off towards the bathroom. "I'm leaving for breakfast in a half hour. With or without you!"

I close my eyes, open them back up again, and Helms is standing over me, showered, shaved, and dressed for the day.

"Now ya got ten minutes."

I get up and take a quick glance into a frightened dresser mirror. I can barely see my island tan through the green. Shower time. I've seen better fleshtones on week-old produce. It's cold in the hallway and, I might add, it's cold in London. I mean frigid, the hallway's like a goddam morgue. I can't believe that people live like this all the time. It's cold. It's dank. It's drafty. No wonder everyone around here always looks like they just got dunked in a sweat bath. I run down the hall in a threadbare towel until I come to the bathroom, which I expect to be steamy and toasty, but of course I'm brutally mistaken. The bathroom has a goddam breeze blowing through it. I could fly a kite in the place if the ceiling was a foot higher!

The morning shower is sacred to me—one ritual that knows no prejudice. 8 to 80, blind, crippled, or crazy, doesn't everyone get a couple minutes of steamy solitude? Silky beads of water rolling down the old back. Comfort. A few minutes of peace before it's time to go out into the day and realize that those days of yesteryear, doing the Huck Finn thing down at the local sewer-steam, were the best days. I mean shower—the point at which life falls into a coma. My head says, "Womb, asshole! Say WOMB!" But I'm not gonna pretend to remember what it was like in the womb. I might still FEEL it, but it isn't a thing I can TELL you about. The shower is quiet compared to the sounds I hear every day, like logs on the fire that burns inside my head, raging, sometimes a whisper, but always burning. Sometimes I think if I had an X ray of my brain, all it would show is a few goldfish flopping around on a cold, cold floor, yelling something about fast food, saying something about swimming again. I just want to know what cartoon did it to me. I mean how did it happen? Was it something I ate as a kid, or what? Too many Lucky Charms, with all those marshmallows making me restless? I'm not bitter about it. I just wanna know. It's the age-old and completely laughable question, "What's it all about?" that I seem to be dancing around. Or was I dancing around a windy bathroom in London? Is it all about my dick? Does everything have to make me feel nervous, stupid, or horny? I had a boss who used to say, "It's all about your dick, Jimi. Unless you're a queer, and then, it's all about my dick." The shower is just so crucial to all of this. To all of these things that amaze and paralyze THE ME.

The bathroom, meanwhile, is a mess. I think basically somebody got so cold that they tried to start a fire and now all that's left is a huge black hole with a ring around it. There isn't even a tub left, it's just a ring. And the worst part? The worst part is that there isn't even a standard shower. Just this thing Londoners call a "Sha-bath," or maybe it's that the process is called "Sha-bathing." I don't know. I don't think the thing even deserves its own name. Let's face it, it's a nozzle with a hose at the end of it, and that's it! A cheap rubber hose with a fuckin' lousy little nozzle at the end of it. No one should feel like they're doing something that merits its own term when they hold this hose and beg for a decent spray from its puny prudish mouth. I don't think the

Limeys have the guts to come clean on this one! They can't admit that, even though they've had a country for centuries, they never managed to come up with a decent shower. It's not even usable! How's a guy supposed to rinse, and lather, and relax, and benefit from the pulsating stream, and masturbate, all at the same time? It's too much work! I can't be bothered with all this HAND-HELD stuff! I'm trying to get a little relief, a little bit of a rush before I go out to face the sharks, and I gotta hold my own shower head. It just doesn't make sense. It might sound primitive, even ridiculous, but it's me and the facts are the facts! It's just too much to do at once! I need that thing up on a hook. Christ, they figured out how to make lamps, what's so difficult about a shower? Imagine trying to spank the old monkey under the covers, while flipping through a porn holding a lightbulb. That shit'd be dangerous! Why's the shower so different?

Anyways, so I'm laying in this filthy bathtub. I got this stupid nozzle in my hand, which is starting to cramp up on me, and I'm pulling hard 'cause I got a strong wind at my back. The ambiance alone has my cock purple and huffing, not to mention the watering it's getting. Like it's a posy I'm wishing over. Coaxing it to grow, begging it to become something it isn't. I almost wish one of my new feline housemates would walk in on me. I must look kind of stud-like with my Popeye forearm and my flared nostrils. I could ask her to light me up a cigarette or something. If she really cared about me, she could hold the nozzle. My arm's so cramped, I'm gonna need occupational therapy when it's all over. It's all just a little bit too weird for me, and it makes me think that either I overemphasize the importance of my morning shower, or I just don't know where to beat off on THIS side of the Atlantic. It shouldn't be so much work. I pulled a lot of muscles. I'm no Houdini! It's finally over. I let out a raging whimper, jump up, grab my towel, make a quick sign of the cross, and take my chances in a dead run back down the hall.

I look in Doobe's drawer and find a nice stash of boxer shorts. The sock pickings are slim but they'll do. I haven't told Doobe that I forgot socks and underwear. It's my little secret and the longer it stays that way the better. I brought two pairs of jeans: a black pair and my favorite old blues, like soft baby flannel. I put the blues on. My ass definitely looks better in the blues. I reach into my duffel and fish out a T-shirt. Black, perfect, always maintain the Johnny Cash color code, my sister says. I fell in love with a girl who worked for Chanel when I was 19, and I've been lookin' like a lost episode of *Dark Shadows* ever since. I give myself a good dose of Vaseline on the hair and carve out a fresh pompadour. Yeah, I might look a touch green but it's been working for Keith Richards for years. One last glance in the mirror, just long enough to catch the essence—a quick cut. Zip up the fake Beatle boots and I'm out the bedroom door.

PULP 16

"I was beginning to worry about you . . . Thought maybe you had extensive WRINKLE damage from the shower."

"From that shower? It was all I could do to hang in long enough for a little spank. No wonder everyone looks so greasy and tense around here."

"I don't think they carry the guilt the way we do, Jimi."

Doobe hands me a nice, fat, burning, hash spliff. Its smokey plume is waltzing throughout the entire room. The smell is user-friendly and the feeling is ancient. Each taste of the sweet smoke washes away a little piece of my morning travails. The apartment has high, high ceilings. I hadn't imagined the place would be so big. Most of the rooms have a vacant feel, except for the kitchen. A space filled with travelers. No one's going out to buy curtains or a new couch. The kitchen has some nice italian crockery and a spice rack, all filled, but that's about as homey as it gets. The rest of the pad is done in Mid-Eighties Crack Den.

We sit in the kitchen smoking the spliff while Doobe makes tea. No better way to start the day.

High. It makes the day, the world, glow with a lost promise. Something could happen that's never happened before. A roller-coaster ride in the mind in exchange for a small chunk of the soul. We throw down our tea and Doobe puts out the spliff. "We'll save it for late night. Let's get outta here."

PuLp17

We walk up to the Leland cafe—a generic little hole that somehow reeks of character, in spite of the fact that it looks like it coulda been decorated by monkeys on tranquilizers. This place gives new meaning to the word, "cardboard." There's a fat old lady named Lou who takes the orders and yells them through a window that looks into the kitchen. A table of locals drink tea, yell and eat. I don't see ten teeth between the four of them. Pale as ghosts, with no saving grace other than cool flannel shirts.

"Bloody Lane, I got the tab yesterday and I won't have it again!"

"You're a bloody liar, Johnny . . . Come on now and pull out your end of the bill!"

"Lou darling, could we settle up with you another day?"

"You boys've been settling up tomorrow since you were ten, now come on with it."

Helms orders the special and I follow suit. An egg, toast, beans, a rasher of bacon, chips and tea. Helms gets a side of black pudding—butcher scraps and blood all fried up together. I pass on the pudding but agree to taste Doobe's and I've got to admit that the shit isn't all that bad as long as I don't think too specifically about its origins. We bury our faces in our plates, stopping only occasionally to ask for salt or pepper. The "special" is thrown on the plate with no concern for esthetics. The beans are everywhere but the quality is there and the hash's got me hungry. I'm eating so fast that I'm out of breath and I feel destined for a bad case of the hiccups. Breakfast at the Leland is good.

Before I know it, we're outside the pub again—Lally's, where we finished off last night. Sitting next to a couple of young skate-nazis and their pit bull, swilling on a rich dark beer. With every gulp, I think less of the vicious dog next to me. My throat is desperate for long sips of beer. English ale is full—chocolate cake with opium icing. A big red double-decker comes chugging up the street.

"Down with it, Jimi boy . . . We can't waste this good ale."

I've never been much of a beer chugger, even though I was a fraternity boy, but the prospect of leaving behind this good ale inspires me. It'd be like pissing on the Bible. So down the hatch and off on the double-decker. My life is becoming more of a middle-class postcard every minute.

We wind through the streets of South London.

I'm knee-deep in history I never read and I'm filled with good beer, black hash and the Leland Special. The streets are jagged and the bus has to snake its way through every turn, inching along, taking its time. The bus has a certain respect for the streets. I don't mind at all. It gives me time to see the world outside. Doobe's quiet and I just watch. It's a working-class neighborhood. Nothing to get too excited about. It's the part I love. It's not that I'm all down-home, or that I relate all that much to my fellow man. I just like to see what the nowheres look like. I give little imaginary histories to it all, mostly the people. Who they love and where they work and how they sleep and what kind of face they make when they fart or come or cry, or die. I LOOK at the people. I look into their eyes. I try to see their pain and their joy. I want to FEEL them. It always makes me sad but I do it anyway. I wanna taste the ham they ate last night. I wanna read the mail that comes everyday in all the colorful little mailboxes. I wanna see the schools. I wanna see the hottest girl in the neighborhood, the toughest guy in the neighborhood. It's my fantasy. I wanna see the houses of the rich and I wanna see the street corners that the hoods and dealers hang out on. All the things that don't change. All the things that make up the world. It's alright seeing the famous places, but it's the non-points of interest that interest me the most. I like them the best.

The houses are all brick. Everything in London is

so fucking bricky, with wood trim painted all different colors, just like the mailboxes, and none of the windows are the same shape. Some window guy probably made a fortune in this town. I look at each and every house, and I think there's a world hidden inside them all—an epic. I wanna pair of X-ray glasses so I can watch them all unfold. I could look at all the naked ladies: their curves, their smiles, their hips, as they look at themselves alone in the mirror, beautiful. Every house is a stage, and on it is a comedy, and a tragedy, and a romance, and a lot of in-between stuff. Yeah, a lot of in-between stuff.

We arrive at Victoria Station and I gotta piss bad. I can't think about anything but pissing. I'd blow off Armageddon if I had to drain my bladder. It drives me crazy and it makes me miserable. I can't enjoy life with pissing on my mind. Life is a hassle until I find a bathroom, or even better, an alley. I like the wind.

I find a bathroom and I pull out my rig. "Oh yes! I can smile again!" I look up at the ceiling and I push my hips in towards the stall. Happy thoughts! I can go on if I don't have the pressure welling up inside of me. Life is beautiful again! Just a couple of minutes, and I see the world in a different way. A golden stream splashing back off the side of the urinal. I wonder how many times I'll piss in my life. Or how many countries I'll piss in. The hot steamy back splash occasionally grazes my steering hand. It's nothing I can't wash off. It's nothing that isn't worth the trouble.

Pulp18

So Doobe tells me I gotta have a tube pass to get around London.

"Look, I don't have the dough for it," I tell him.

"I'll buy it for you . . . All you gotta do is pose for the picture."

"Pose . . . No problem." I give it my best pout—distant, melancholy, intense, all while sucking my cheeks in. Brando'd be proud. The pass gives me free rein within city limits. We walk out of the station and run smack dab into Westminister Abbey. Its tall steeple shooting up into the sky, just short of God. The tall gothic shit and old Ben and all the double-deckers everywhere and all the color and the Thames and the bridges and all of it—real heavy tourist stuff. Old movie type, like where's Rex Harrison in all of this shit. I'm overcome. I don't know whether to beat off, get drunk, eat a candy bar or just be afraid. I, me, Jimi Banks, am part of human history! Part of the history of this fucking world. I look around and I feel it. King fucking Tut and me! I'm in a place that means something. I wanna celebrate. I want to remember it forever like a big collage of lights and sounds and colors and laughter and tears and fear and never being the way I think it's gonna be. I hear music—rock and roll but big, like symphonies with flutes and drums and violins and summers and candy and all the girls I ever loved. Little pieces. My whole life in little pieces. I never get to remember the whole thing at once. I just get little pieces. Trapped in a postcard, inside a cartoon, waving to the camera.

I follow Helms, a few steps behind the whole way. He goes that New York way—running the whole time even when he's walking. We cross the Thames and drop down under a stone bridge to the side of the National Theatre at the South Bank. There's a pub right on the side of the Theatre. These people aren't afraid. They got pubs everywhere! America! We're so afraid of everything. So afraid of being sued, so afraid of neighbors, so afraid of queers, so afraid of dykes, and drugs, nudity, sex, murder, incest, rape, life, our fathers, loving our mothers, and most of all . . . FEAR. So fucking afraid to be afraid! Ever since that one jerk wrote "Sinners in the Hands of an Angry God," we've all been so fucking scared! Me included! I still can't believe those little lame pilgrims cried when he read that stupid sermon in church. Wherever it was, probably Boston—the lamest place in America. Liberal town . . . Yeah, right!

A pub at the National Theatre, what a beautiful thing. Let's face it, no one could use a few drinks like all the pretentious weasels who roam through museums, pretending to FEEL and KNOW what the artist meant. They analyze and they hypothesize and they intellectualize and they yearn to fuck and wish they knew and want to be but don't have the time because they're too busy smoking weird, bad-smelling cigarettes and writing long boring papers and . . . Call me fucking Ishmael!

We go inside the little woody outhouse-like tavern and Helms orders us a few ciders. Nice. Tastes like fine wine-beer. It may be the best morning lager known to man. I could easily see myself becoming a cider junky and never being able to go back to the U.S.A.

Back outside, we grab seats at a table. I smile and I look over at Doobe. He's smiling too. Unspoken and True. A Moment of Communication. The words only ever fill up the holes. Sitting in the Shade of Life. Five minutes of easy, five minutes of no death, no family, no job, no dick, freedom! Freedom from my dick and all its demands! Big Ben over us and I can feel it ticking. The Pulse of this Little World.

"Jimi, what did you do while all the shit went down with Ray?"

"I talked a lot of shit about it. AT IT, mostly. It's like I'm watching a movie of my life and he dies. I think I'm only fucking PLAYING at it."

The sun is in and out of the picture and I hear the horns above me on the bridge. I feel like a person on a planet, standing on the edge of a huge ball of rock and dirt. Sitting and thinking and being in a conversation that takes me away from any real connection. Half in a strange place and half in a little white wooden chapel on Long Island with a bunch of people I went to school with listening to some repressed minister talk about a Ray. Poor bastard, how shitty does it feel to stand in front of a crowd of people, talking about someone they knew when you didn't even know him. Trying to console them with your godly words about how it WAS SOMETHING, when it just WAS. I tried to see him. I tried to see him above the crowd, dancing his silly dead-head dance. I tried to see him, happy, I wanted to see him happy at that point. I wanted to believe that he had come to terms with what went down, with his death.

"Yeah . . . I was over here in the land of civilized chill. I told a few people about it, but it just seemed so far away . . . It was good to go back and see the people who knew him . . . It's good to see you, Jimi." He takes a sip of his cider.

"Yeah, well I wasn't doin' anything anyways. Jimi, I kinda wonder, you know . . . What the fuck ever happened to the dude?"

"I don't know . . . I think sometimes it's a jump and a skip away from all of us. A simple fucking hopscotch."

"You think?"

"I think. I guess. I know. His blue neck might've saved mine." I look up and I see a few Sid Vicious look-alikes walking in front of us. One of them has a pet rat on his shoulder. "Doobe, don't you ever just wanna say FUCK IT and jump?"

"I don't know. I haven't really ever thought it through."

"He did."

PuIp19

I've never been a nightclub Mozart. If a woman likes me and she isn't a total pig and she makes the slightest effort to lasso me . . . Bingo . . . She's got me. The only problem might be that I won't get the hint. I'm easy and I'm lonely. I need to make a phone call, but first I need to jump back three months and remember something out loud from the Suburban Peep Show Getto that is my mind.

It all starts back on the island with me tending bar by the beach with black shorts on and my hair slicked back in a high-sheen pompadour. I meet this british dude, Rolland. Now, Rolland is a Gin Freak and it's my job to give him drinks for his tables 'cause he's a walter. Walters have to be drunk to be good. It's the only way to tend to nightmarish people all night long and still maintain a good sense of humor. It takes a certain ego not to feel insulted by the demands of the average customer: the water, the napkins, the raw steak that isn't rare enough, the burnt pork chop that still may harbor disease. I get tipped out by him and I find out that he's a gin lush so I start feeding him drinks while he works. All over the place, he can't get enough by the end of the night. I gotta remind him to give his tables checks because he's so into his own martinis. Rolland has a friend named Diane who comes to see him one night. Fate is on my side as I see a pair of long ivory tusks that have found their way onto the bottom half of a woman. Diane digs me from the get-go, she starts coming up every night to visit Rolland and we do the eye thing. Rolland comes over to me with his drunken british giggle and puts in the word.

"Jimiiiii . . . Oh Jimiiii . . . My friend Diane has quite a crush on you!" But I'm scared because I love Lindsey. I'm scared because I'm falling prey to Diane. My penis is telling me that love is not an issue. It's straining my tighty whiteys and telling me that opportunity's knocking and deep down in my flesh-loving heart . . . I just can't pass it up. I'm a slave. I could be giving Marilyn Monroe's fleshy ghost the bone and I woulda still had to give it to Diane.

ENTER THE ULTERIOR MOTIVE.

Blond and tan with a short pixie-type hairdo and those legs I mentioned and little pert titties and cute teeth and lips that purr and freckles and the british accent. I think her hands were even beautiful. I don't think she had a flaw other than the fact she liked to fuck other girls' guys, but doesn't everybody? A Divine Form of Rape. The oldest form of human sport, maybe animal even? Lord of the Flies Meets the Devil in Miss Jones.

So finally, one night, I can't take it anymore. I can't bear to think that there's a totally hot chick within arm's reach who wants me and I'm not doing anything about it. I have to make my move. It doesn't matter whether or not I'm in love. I have to take my chance and try to hang with this woman. I'm in the bathroom of the bar, washing my hands and staring at my face in the mirror. I flash a quick-copied smile and wink with sure-bet confidence. Diane's sipping on a white wine spritzer or something and I lay down my rap. I mean, of course I'm confident, the girl has all but demanded that I ask her out.

"Diane, would you like to take a trip up island tomorrow?"

"Jimi? . . . Are you SURE you can make the time for me?"

"Of course I can . . . I do what I want," I roar with a hand through my hair.

"Oh I forgot," she laughs. ". . . Your own man."

I'm even as bold as to tell Lindsey what I'm gonna do, "Yeah. Hey don't worry, baby, we're just friends and I want to show her the island. I love you, you know that, don't worry . . . I'll be back for dinner."

I want to be honest and give my conscience a break. It's noble and besides . . . Lindsey knows Diane has the hots for me. Diane's my ace in the hole. What I don't realize at the time is that aces in the hole are only good as long as they're kept in the HOLE. I've heard that it's better to have loved and lost but I always seem to lose FIRST and then LOVE.

I meet Diane on the other side of the island and we grab a quick bite at a skeasy fishing bar—half off on drinks for every green tooth you flash. Clam chowder and fat greasy burgers. We wash it down with nice scotch on the rocks. Diane is a woman of breeding. Her father's an ambassador on some obscure island that the british still consider part of their empire. I can't be anything more than her ugly american fling—her polished peasant. She hangs out with like composers and watercolorists and other really sensitive skeeks who wear cufflinks and cologne and have houses on the water, and all I have is a pretty nice pair of Ray•Bans and a few funny lines.

The thing I do got goin' for me is the eyes. She really digs the eyes and believe me, I work it hard. She told me once that I had "deep piercing eyes," so every time I see her now, I give her these wild intense stares and pretend I don't even know I'm doing it. Like I'm looking deep into her soul, like my eyes are tiny cameras. Yeah . . . She really seems to go for that.

After lunch, we jump into my jeep and head up island. At the head of the island, there are these huge cliffs with mud baths at the bottom, where couples can frolic naked and paint each other with mud.

We climb down the cliffs and go for a quick swim. I don't have anything on and all Diane has on is a skimpy pair of bikini bottoms. It's hard to keep my dick from being anything other than icecicular, but I'm not sure where I stand at this point and it's never really too suave to run around a nude beach with a hard-on. So instead, I conjure up what I think is a negative fantasy about the pervert janitor that used to watch us boys shower in high school. Remembering his fat, sweating, pimply mug drooling over us while we toweled off after hockey practice was enough to hold my genitalia at bay while Diane and I casually floated out past the waves. Diane has the classic pert little titties. Her nipples look like tiny pink periscopes surfacing after each wave rolls by. I start to swim under her . . . Testing . . . I'm met with no resistance. Most guys would know by now that everything is A-OK, but not me . . . Somehow I never know where I'm at with the women.

Ten minutes later, in spite of it all, we're kissing, covered head to toe in mud . . . Then we're down in the water . . . Then we're back up in the mud . . . On the beach . . . Back into the water . . . Up in the mud—for what seems like hours . . . Or seconds. Until finally, we climb high above the water, above the mighty Atlantic and I sandwich Diane between a huge jagged rock and the side of the cliff, and we commence to fucking.

Power rushes through our bodies . . . Trembling . . . Sweating . . . Straining to keep upright on the cliffside. We must be a 100 feet above the water . . . No, I take that back . . . 200 and that's when it all hits me! The sun beating down on us, Diane's pussy all warm and wet like a bowl of velvet oatmeal, I think to myself, "Could this be it? I got Lindsey at home—the girl is like some buxom 1950s Playboy Bunny and I got this lanky british girl riding me into total oblivion 1000 feet above the ocean . . . I pour booze for top dollar on Paradise Island . . . What else could there be?" I close my eyes and I pray. I pray to God to strike me dead with preferably a golden lightning bolt . . . I don't wanna go on . . . How many moments like this does a guy get in a lifetime? Maybe the next fifty years is all about bad jobs . . . And fat chicks . . . And debt . . . And broken dreams . . . And tough breaks? How much better could it be?

PULP 20

So like I was sayin', off to the phone booth. Lindsey, by the way, did find out about Diane . . . Really. There's a broken phone outside the pub where everyone calls everyone they've ever known from all over the world. I get in line. The line to use the phone is long and, after a little while, I decide that I can't wait any longer, even though the phone is free. When people have a chance to call anywhere in the world for as long as they want, for free, they talk for a long time. I got four people in front of me and

I figure it's gonna be months before I get to touch that clammy receiver. The guy on the phone doesn't look like he's going anywhere in the next hour or so, so I fish out a few pieces of change and I go over to the other phone. Diane has a house in "the country" and I figure I got enough change to cover the fare. I take a gamble and I dial. Diane said she'd be at "Mum's" and if she isn't, then she'll get the message. I fire a coin into the phone and I'm met with jeers from the others waiting in line. They're offended . . . Like I don't have the balls to wait it out with them! My rationale howls a different tune. I figure it's so completely inevitable that I'm gonna run out of cash, why get bogged down by a few lousy coins. The only people who worry about money are the people who work for it, need it, or don't have any friends who'll lend it to them. I don't fit into any of those categories. I got a list, etched into the last few cells of my brain, of all the people left who'll lend me a few shekels. I can throw away some change. Yeah . . . I can blow money. It makes me feel good. It makes me feel free, like I'm winning the game in my own small way. The only way I can change The Game is to be out of the game. I can't care too much about the little piece I cling to. I don't have much and I'm losing small parts of that "much" all the time. As long as things are working out, as long as life is good . . . I won't take too many gambles. Conventional success'll kill my soul. If the women are throwing themselves at me, and there's money in the bank, and people are digging my scene and the hair looks good . . . There's nowhere to go but down. Who wants to lose the condo and the BMW because of a new wrong haircut or bad, bad shoes? The fear'll keep me on the treadmill. The inspiration hides out in the head, bouncing, careening like any other ping-pong ball. I got a few more loans left in the cosmic bank and they . . . they're all that's holding me back from yet another reinvention, yet another comeback for Jimi! The sooner I give away my last few pennies and burn my last bridge, the better off I'll be. So really . . . I'm not putting change into a phone . . . I'M MAKING ROOM FOR MY FUTURE!

Diane isn't home so I leave a message with her mother . . . But I walk away proud.

I walk into the pub. Helms is sitting at a table, staring out the window, running his hand through his curly locks, stopping only to occasionally scratch his chin. The table's got a small green towel on it to soak up the spilled suds—it advertises one of the local scotches. A pair of frothy pints sit next to each other, swapping foam. I sit down and take a long pull, like poison coal to a furnace. Washing away thoughts of Lindsey . . . And Ray . . . And my parents . . . Anything I didn't have a ready-made answer for. I'm not sure whether seeing Diane would remind me of Lindsey, or help me to forget her. I look out the window of the pub onto the Strand—one of those famous british streets. I remember one of my college profs telling us a story about Charles Dickens and he mentioned the Strand. The story escapes me, as does most of college . . . A stop in time . . . A four-year freeze . . . A reading list . . . A bag of Ecstasy . . . A month of therapy.

It starts to rain and rain is just perfect for London, for who I am, and what I'm doing. It works over here. A town like L.A. looks like a been-around-the-block-too-many-times and won't-ya-come-home-with-me kind of bleach-blonde, pussy-haired, really . . . I'm-not-HIV-positive sort of street-walkin' whore when it rains, but London wears it well . . . Its mascara doesn't run. The people walk faster and some even run. They all have umbrellas and if they don't, they buy newspapers. I hear a sad trumpet, or maybe a lonely cornet. The brick gets cleaner with every drop that hits it and the people keep on running . . . I think about this and that. I let Lindsey creep back in even though I don't want to but it doesn't hurt that much because I'm here . . . And she's there . . . And I won't see her today. I look at Doobe and I'm happy that I wasted four years in college just because I met Doobe. I think about Ray and I wish he were here. I wish my brother Ray were here . . . I wish he were here. The rain falls and falls and everyone hurries for shelter. The bustle. I could watch it forever from a bar, three steps below street level, but I never want to be a part of it unless I have it my way. I'll hide and bide. I'm afraid to jump into that big pond. I take a drag of my beer. They tell me it feels good for them to work. That it fills their days and their minds. I'm happy sitting here with a pocket full of borrowed money and a head full of rain.

PULP 21

"So tell me what happened to Lindsey."

"I met Lindsey at the beginning of the summer. We hung for a couple of weeks and then, BOOM . . . She's living with me and everything is perfect. We're renting a room from the Good Witch and everybody seems happy. I got a case of the herpes that I got left over from the summer before and I tell Lindsey about it and we vow to be careful. Of course, one morning I wake up and slip a sleep-eyed bone into her and BAM . . . She's got it for life. I get the sinking feeling in my stomach and so does she. Doobe, the herpes can drop an atomic bomb on passion, lemme tell ya that. The blossoming romance became more of a dying cactus in the Arctic and that was it. I couldn't get over it . . . Even more so than her, I think."

"Did she leave you then?"

"No, she stayed . . . I came home one day . . . It musta been about noon and I was out of my mind. I can't even remember where I had been . . . But wherever it was, there was plenty of bourbon and I was deep into it. I told her I wanted to have sex and she said OK. We went into our bedroom and the next thing I know . . . I'm staring at the wall next to my bed with demon eyes, pounding my fists against the wall as hard as I can and Lindsey's yelling for me to stop. I stop and I drop back into bed and then I tell her that I want to make love and she says, 'We just did . . . Don't you remember pounding into me for forty-five minutes before you passed out?' I started to hug her. I wanted to cry. I didn't really know what to do or say though . . . Yeah . . . That was pretty much how it went from there. The best I could do was like . . . rape her in a blackout."

It's late in the afternoon and things are getting blurred and profound after a long day's drinking. The pints are chilly. The bartender's looking at us with pained disgust. He's one of those postmodern Elvis types with big pork chop sideburns and a high, high head of hair, curly. It's more of a late-life Elvis look, circa Rhinestones and White Cape. We're his nightmare on this particular day. There's always somebody. Doobe's up on his stool calling for whiskey. I'm laughing and telling my version of my life story. Doobe keeps bumping this tough guy next to him and the tough guy's getting all frumpy. I start to think that maybe the tough guy isn't quite as tough as he's dressed. Unfortunately for him, Doobe is too swirvy to regard his store-bought Eastwood. A VICIOUS CYCLE. Doobe bumps the guy . . . And the guy gets all ruffled . . . And then Doobe buys him a shot . . . They drink it . . . There's an apology, and then, it happens all over again—

Doobe's distraught equilibrium is bigger than his heart.

PULP 22

A group of people walk into the bar, point at Doobe and come towards us, even though he's completely oblivious to their entrance. Three of them—two guys and a girl.

"Helms, I almost bloody missed you while I was gone!" says a beanpole with freckles and a firebush coiff.

"Donald," Helms slurps. "This is my buddy, Jimi, from the States."

"You're the bloody Yank who wakes me up at all hours of the morning ringing up Helms. I thought you'd be older the way you talk so bloody slow . . . Sound like you're on your bloody deathbed when you call!"

"It's he-red-i-tary."

"Well, if that's the bloody case, then I hope your parents don't call while you're here 'cause I'm SURE they'll call in the middle of the night and I'm sure they'll talk even SLOWER! I got bloody bags under my eyes from you!"

Everything is a crisis when Donald speaks—Woody Allen, but less anal and more snob. He forgets me and goes back to his counterparts, hands looping madly, eyebrows aquiver, voice jumping.

". . . So I'm up in the bloody tree and I'm hanging by one bloody arm and Mum is under me, picking up the fallen apples. 'Mum, I'm bloody about to drop! I can't hold on any longer!' and she's saying, 'Just a minute, Deary. Let me gather up these last few.' I couldn't bloody believe it! I'm about to fall from God knows how many feet and Mum's treating me like a bloody wanker!"

Every once in awhile, he breaks from his story, "I'm so BLOODY DRUNK, MY GOD!" and goes on ranting. I get right into the flow of the story, drawn to the urgency, unaware of the details.

With Donald come Linda and Louis. Linda, also a redhead, has a luscious, bursting pair of raisin-tipped breasts. A little on the heavy side, but no matter, her person nullified any shortcomings whatsoever. She sat next to me with a warmth that called my leather onto the back of my chair. If I didn't need a showpiece arm trophy to feel like a man, I would've asked her to marry me on the spot. My LOVE is mercurial and my LUST paves the way. Linda looks at me and smiles with such honesty that I'm struck speechless, not knowing which of my personas to assume.

"How ya doin'?" I stutter, in my best city-speak.

"Fine, Jimi," climbing over my oral shield. "You're a cute boy, aren't you."

That does it! BOY . . . CUTE BOY! Like a homing pigeon on my Oedipal G-spot! The romance begins to bloom in my head. Dinner at Her favorite London spot, hand-kissing walks along Henry Moore sculpture-dotted brick walkways. Inside my head roams a TRUE ROMANTIC. I just coat it with a fallen rock-god shell to fool myself.

Louis stands up at the bar waiting for an ale, occasionally darting Liberace eyes over at my fidgety groin. One glance at his blood-colored riding suit, complete with leather crop and shaved head, and I feel like a 12-year-old runaway looking for Huck Finn in Times Square on a Saturday night, his dark chocolate skin only adding to the confusion of my deepest naughty slave fantasies.

"Well, enough about me and Mum . . . Whatta ya say we go on outside and smoke this spliff?" Donald whistles, producing a bloated spliff.

"I wish we had bloody X . . . That's what I'd like for work tonight . . . Wouldn't you, Helms?" my redhead vixen says.

"I'd love X . . . I need something to pick me up," he answers.

"Helms, you didn't tell me you had to work tonight," I say.

"I hadn't thought about it in a coupla hours."

"Enough bloody talk about it, let's go and smoke this bloody spliff I got before Linda and Doobe have to go in to work."

We walk out into the alley behind the bar. Louis follows, sipping a tall ale. "I'm going to get all wet in this rain!" He shrieks. The sweet smoke umbrellas us from the rain as much as we need it to. It's still light out, but the day is in its final desperate encore. The city glows around its edge—a sad window into the past, a childhood I never let myself have, a first love I can't remember, parents I ran from, a sister who didn't like me because I was spoiled, a perspective I won in a lottery. I give it all back. I throw it away with every hit of hash that dances in my head. I get no family and all the fleeting support I need in return. When the spliff is gone, Doobe and Linda run off to wait tables and I return inside with Donald and Louis to have another beer. It's decided that we'll go and cop X while Linda and Doobe toss grub to theatergoers at Joe Allen—dramaland eatery that it is. I've never heard of the place, but then again, you don't catch me sashaying down Broadway very often either.

"I'll get you a pint, Honey!" giggles Louis when I cry a fake poor. I'm tempted to ask "of what," but refrain, seeing potential in the relationship. Donald and I grab a new table while Louis grabs the pints and Donald resumes telling me about his stay with Mum. The crowd has begun to thin out in the pub.

"We'll drink these down quick and go over to Robyn's house. She's got good bloody X and if you catch her in a decent mood, she'll bloody give it to you!" Donald confides. Louis returns with fresh pints from the bar and I turn the head back on autopilot.

Pulp 23

The rain's gone home for the evening, leaving behind a chill. We walk through the streets. I feel at ease in these anonymous streets watching and listening to Louis and Donald. The lamplight's warm. Faces hurry past, flickering out of the shadows only for an instant.

"Hurry up now, Honey! He walks just like he talks . . . Slow, heeheehee," Louis says to Donald, up in front of me. They turn the corner, I speed up, following their chatty heads as we cut through Leicester Square.

"Robyn's flat's just on the other side of the square," Donald says, with a long arm pointing at a small building. There's a fortune-teller's half-mooned shop on the ground level and a man holding a baby while talking on the phone in the window up above the flower boxes, in between white wooden shutters.

"Christian . . . Oh Christian, my love . . ." Louis yells up at the window. ". . . He's almost as cute as you, Jimi."

"He IS a real looker isn't he," I squirm, half sarcastically, half jealous. The door next to the shop buzzes open. We wind up a tight staircase and into the flat.

The flat's painted gold with a dull black ceiling and there's industrial music playing loud. Christian holds the baby in his arms while he argues on the phone and circles the entire flat. We sit down in the living room and Donald pulls out another spliff. The beat of the music cuts through the room—a mix of power tools, synthesizers and chemical anger. Mannequins, painted all different colors, hang from the ceiling—black ones, blue ones, ones with glitter. The walls are filled with paintings and sketches all of the same model.

"Oh that's Robyn . . . She's a real Madonna fan, heeheehee!" Louis says, noticing that I'm drawn in by the similarity of all the pictures. Robyn has a sexuality about her. I don't know if it's the artwork or the premise but the point gets across. I sit back, take a hit of the passed spliff while she watches me from all over the room . . . Purring . . . Secrets from another lifetime. She's OF some other century . . . I guess would be the best way to imprison her in the written word. More a damsel than a woman. It would be alright to tell her what I really thought and felt. She would know it anyways. The old man once told me that french women were as old as their country, not as their cunts, and I can see the story of England etched into Robyn's oil-base eyes. Not brash and new, like American bitches, all attitude and no wisdom. But pools of sin, deep and warm, her eyes tell me. The kind of sin that stands above judgment, quietly commanding respect.

"This Robyn chick already HAS everything Madonna's got."

". . . And more, heeheehee!" Louis and Donald both sing.

Christian and the baby now stand in front of us.

"Robyn's due back any minute." He walks back out of the room into the hallway. The baby looks at us over Christian's shoulder with silent eyes. Christian's striking, with hard angles and olive skin like some Apache or something. One of those weird post-modern model types. The baby looks like it could be his. Donald gets up and walks into the kitchen, returning with 3 pints of ale. We all take swigs and sit drowning in the pulse and bang of the techno-grunge muzak. The flat spooks me . . . Drug vibe . . . I can taste the bad energy in the beer. This place's got a black soul. I'm uneasy and restless even though I'm drawn to all the Robyns.

"Robyn broke that bed buggering Christian with a bloody strap-on," Donald says, pointing to a broken-down bed in the corner of the room.

"Didn't you, Christian?" Louis chirps.

"What?" He looks up from the phone, irritated, the child ducking behind his shoulder.

"I said didn't YOU and Robyn break THAT bed with nasty toys?" Louis repeats, pulling a huge black strap-on dildo out of a table drawer. "Have this tagged and marked as a divine weapon, heeheehee!" he titters.

"Put that bloody thing away, would you, Louis! I got a sore backside just looking at it!" Donald says. Christian is out of sight by now, off in the kitchen. I sit with this twisted Laverne and Shirley and wait for the X-Damsel. The music marches on with the clang of hammers, the shrieks of tortured keyboard, and every once in awhile, a vocal comes on and says something like, ". . . You are not alone . . . I cry . . . We fuck!" I love industrial music. It captures something in me that I can't quite grasp alone in a bathtub . . . It really does. Sitting in this apartment listening to the theme song of the death row chain gang moving through a toxic jungle after an acid rain, banging and building a road to hip-hop nowhere, running alongside a pair of tittery London Paul Lynne sound-alikes.

Sounds from the street fill up the front window. Every once in awhile, a cry earns the right to be part of the tribal mega-symphony—loud enough and angry enough to filter into the picture. Searing horns, nursed by double-decker engines straining, muted cries, footsteps fast and hard, keep time true down in the square. Dinner's calling for everyone, including my trio. We're holding out for the chemical option. I take another drag off the spliff. I'm still not used to the tobacco mixed with the hashish. It makes me uneasy. I'm rushed. The couch is too soft and I'm sinking into it, drowning in the lint of a thousand drug deals. I look around for a wooden chair to save me. I jump up and begin to circle the room, pretending to study the acrylic veneer of the mannequins, checking the frayed nooses that secure them into the ceiling.

No one in the room is speaking. Music rules any conversational attempts there might be. I pace silently, tied down and tortured in my cerebral sofa. A single chirp runs the industrial gauntlet and I look up at a tree that runs alongside the window, a lone blackbird jumping about on its skeletal limbs. I walk over to the glass as other birds begin to congregate on the limbs of the tree. They're chirping, looking into the flat. They look at me and babble on. Are they compelled to swarm this fucking distorted den? Do they yearn to stroke this evil? I look at Donald and Louis, staring off—blank pages. Christian moves in and out of the room like a two-legged cock priming a cesspool . . . Needing a taste of the bitter . . . To be part of the ceremony of lifeless mannequins and golden walls and the music . . . I'm in a trance. The birds shriek and scream. I look at the baby slung over Christian's shoulder, helpless, looking at me, silent. I'm afraid to look back up at him. The night is black by now and the streets are dying down except for an occasional scream. Only the birds. It's all the fucking blackbirds.

"CHEEEEEEEEEEEEEEEEEEEE...CHEEEEEEEEEEE EEEEEEEEEEEEEEEEE...CHEEEEEEEEEEEEEEE!"

Wrenching me, every muscle coiling on my neck with each scream! Gathering still. No one in the room looking at the window but me. The birds know, they know about the drugs and the sodomy. They smell it and they love it. They smell us. We smell it and we love it. I smell it and I love it and I hate myself for it. Deep down, I can't take it. I hate the rooms where I live! Unfocused and drawn into the void. Music shouts under the birds, careening off every wall, off every chair, invading me and raping every ritual mannequin. Laying them down on their sides and fucking them. The sky above the tree, deep red, crying yellow and orange tears. The birds drawing ropes around the muted face of the sky and landing back on the withering tree. I take it all personally, so stupid to think it's my world and they're making me feel wrong. Not letting me breathe . . . Or smile . . . Or laugh anymore! The birds begin to grow in front of my eyes. Each bird swelling, feathers shedding for scales, teeth surge under cracking beaks. Shrieks turn to howls and finally, growls. Lindsey . . . My anger turning outward and rising up in flying beasts. Coming down to me, crashing in through the window. Time stops, Donald and Louis frozen, Christian and the lost babe gone from my sight. Ray's corpse drawn up into the sky by vultures of guilt, swooping and diving. Virus . . . Rotten apples falling down, being grabbed up by lovely children . . . I'm a victim . . . I'm a villain . . . No relief in either . . . Ringing . . . Raging . . . Burning . . . Hissing . . . The birds and my nightmares marry . . . On an altar of my hate . . . Ill-fated gifts awarded on lechery . . . Fucking birds . . . And death . . . Virus . . . And AIDS. Words ring off Lindsey's lips in memory as she wonders. Where are the pirates and princesses of my silly baby dreams? All the places and all the wondering? Am I growing up or am I dying? Were the birds a message singular, taken the form of many? A rush creeps over my body, pulling at my cock and grinding my face into a mass of blood and shredded flesh . . . Seeping . . . They want me . . . I've done the walking and then want to fly me the rest of the way . . . Hissing and . . . Dying. . . .

Christian comes back into the room, irritated.

"Look . . . I don't think she's coming back . . . And I gotta leave. So can you guys just take off?"

I don't even so much as look at Louis or Donald.

"Yeah, good to meet you. I gotta go anyways," and stumble out the door. "See you guys later; thanks for the pints."

I run through the square, lost for about twenty minutes until I find a tube station and jump on a train back to Southfields where the Helms' flat is. Sweating and chilled on the train, feeling good as long as I'm moving. Still hearing the birds, hoping they're only a memory. Not wanting to face anything those fucking birds brought out in me. Just riding the train. Just riding a train through London. . . .

Pulp 24

I'm sitting in the flat, drinking a cup of Drano-strength tea, looking at Sonja and Loren while they play more cards. I stare at their beautiful faces, faces from other ends of the world. Faces of women. Deep in my most primal recesses I need them, and yet, I act as if I could care less. It's my only and weak defense. As if I need a defense, as if they wait for me to like them. Needing the sex, the violence of the act, remembering mostly the beauty. Orgasms abrupt, a shower of lava, soothing, draining rage and frustration. Looking for her to cleanse me. I need to come. It isn't about wanting. I've never had a fucking choice in my life. It's got nothing to do with me. It's him. It's fucking him that isn't satisfied! Lindsey doesn't understand. It's not always about candles and fucking *Bolero*. Scream comes from the hollow, echoing out, lost and crying. I need them.

I listen to the girls talking. Voices delicate, laughter. The way they smoke makes vice an art. Soft between the lips, dangling, then out between thin strong sexy fingers. Fingers that control. I can watch a woman smoke for an hour. I've done it sitting in Washington Square Park with a dollar in my pocket. My last dollar. Listening to the comics and the musicians, deciding who gets the last buck. Who's the greatest artist on New York's streets that day. Watching the girls smoke with gloves on, with hats on. Little berets . . . Watching . . . Staring through sunglasses . . . Watching secretly . . . Watching Loren with her pearly smile.

"So what are you going to do after you take your little holiday?"

"That's a good question, Loren, maybe you could give me an equally good answer as well."

"I'm serious . . . I mean I don't . . . I'm not prying, I mean to say. I was just wondering."

"I know . . . Um . . . I don't know really. After school, I bounced around the States working shitty jobs and basically, I decided that I was tired of working shitty jobs in the States, so I came here."

"That's what we've been doing here for three years. I wish I could give you my job," Sonja adds.

"Yeah, I met Sonja three years ago and we were only going to be here for a summer," laughs, "I'm finally leaving, in a month," laughs, "a five-month safari through Africa. It's taken forever to get out of this place."

"I don't think I've been in a place or a job that I didn't eventually hate . . . And for all the same reasons I hated the job just before it. Routine's just a long spelling for RUT."

"Only four telly stations in this town makes it even tougher."

"Cable TV just prolongs the suffering . . . You're not missing anything over here."

"I can't wait to be in a bloody Land Rover surrounded by huge bloody gorillas!" Loren's always smiling even when she's complaining. Doobe told me that a buddy of his from Greece, Teo, had been hanging out with Loren and that she was still mad about him. Apparently, Teo was one of those guys who could hit a broad in the head with a rock and be fucking her ten minutes later. Loren has one of those double smiles. It's the eyes, like a mirrored looking glass.

So we all agree we've worked too many shitty jobs. Or are we just alive? Is this what had Ray so worked up? He saw his life as an indefinite stint ringing Big Macs up at the local Mickey D's and said, wait a minute? Maybe he wasn't afraid of gods and churches? Maybe he thought of them as banks with lots of benches? And guilt-ridden child molesters with bad tailors?

"It's OK to work shitty jobs as long as you're not living at home. I'd be a waitress anywhere but back home in Sydney."

"Nothing's OK when you're living at home . . . Living at home IS FAILURE!"

We watch the talking heads on TV for awhile. News about dead babies and burning houses and raped women and sick men and all the things that make up reality. Finally, the girls lose interest and go to bed. I stay up and watch TV, figuring all the bad news in the world's got to be better than laying alone in bed, until finally my eyes shut themselves.

The speed, the loudness, I don't have control over any of it anymore. The voices begin to speak their own minds. I'm just watching now while the voices come out of the shadows to dance . . . Watching.

PULP 25

"You know . . . I just never even imagined him all grown up. It's like he wasn't supposed to."

I open my eyes, not quite aware of where I am, then realizing I'm peeling my face off yet another vinyl leisure product. True love again.

"Did you ever see this?" Helms produces a picture from his pocket—Ray sitting in a dried creek bed with his girlfriend, Jane, in what looked to be Colorado. The sun's setting behind them, casting a pair of beam halos over their heads. I'd never seen Ray look the way he looks in the picture. No life, like an empty closet. The only things familiar were the stupid tie-dye socks he always wore for big events. I look at the picture, rubbing eyes, for a minute, and then Doobe hands me a bowl of steaming hashish. I take a hit off the bowl and exhale, thinking that I gotta take a piss. I look up, and Doobe has pulled out a pair of socks. THOSE SAME STUPID SOCKS. I wince at the sight of them, like Doobe's a grave robber or something. Helms looks at me, looks back at the socks, and starts to laugh. "Perfectly good socks," and goes up to bed leaving me with the burning bowl in my hand.

The sky's a thick light blue. The sun's climbing back up above, with tiny beam legs on the edge of the horizon. Another day. I look up at the clock on the wall and its hands tell me it's 5:52. I lay back down, safe in the shadow of the couch, and stare out the window. I watch the sunlight tiptoe up the street, one brick at a time. Time to sleep. . . .

PuIp26

I look into the mirror at the two Xs I call eyes. The thrill of being bloated and green with red blotches is long gone. Living out this cliché and it's killing me. I got a beard that would make Paul Bunyan blush, and I think I'm cool because of a pair of fake Beatle boots. I wear a motorcycle jacket because I had an old jap cycle for about ten minutes. On my arm is a custom-made silver armband that I claim is the sure sign of any "Glamourboy Caveman." I used to be a Little League catcher. And here I am 15 years later looking like one of the extras in *Road Warrior*. I'm living a lie and it's killing me . . . A NEW DAY HAS ARRIVED.

My vision fades in long enough for me to look down and see an uninvited guest—the dreaded boyish nuisance that is THE HERPES. Three small white bubbles have surfaced along the right side of the shaft of my cock. A discovery, musically accompanied by a deep sinking feeling, not totally unlike swallowing a broken Coke bottle. A feeling nurtured and groomed with every careless selfish passing of the virus. Yeah . . . It ain't AIDS . . . But it still sucks! An Eternal Scar. One slip and young lust jumps out a window. The reality of virus, more concrete than love.

Having the herpes after awhile is NO BIG DEAL. Giving the herpes will always suck. In some of my more mock courageous moments, I see it as yet another testament to my beautiful and halfhearted self-destruction. Just another Purple Heart to pin on a suburban grown combat suit. There have even been twisted moments when I envision a whole tribe of gorgeous thirtyish women, frolicking on the beach playing with their newborns, bearing full-length C-section scars—a testimony to OUR passion. Yeah, that's right, brand 'em like cattle then sit back and wait for the Oh-So daunting Judgment Day. The perversion of knowing that a child has to be cut from its mother's body. The tunnel being closed due to disease. Unable to feel, to laugh, to ever be a child again. To ever skip through a supermarket, tagging along mom's shopping cart, singing "Puff the Magic Dragon," to smell a forest, all the trees and flowers, and feel free. Growing up sucks!

Lovers marked like a lecherous deck of cards and me . . . Me . . . Me . . . Me . . . Me . . . Me . . . Me.

I pull out a dull razor from behind the mirror. I begin to scrape the stubble from my face, slowly, with cold water, stopping often to rinse the blade. It hurts. My first pathetic test of the day. A damp towel and one last look. The face looks better. The dick still looks bad. Like a walking Ying-Yang, broken and grooved at the waist.

Pulp 27

"Hullo?"

"Cheers, Jimi!"

"Diane, howya doin'?"

"I wasn't so sure you'd make it over here!" It's too early to be so upbeat but it's good to hear her voice. Immediately, I'm reminded by a squirmy itch that there'll be more lesions sprouting on my penis. Just like a burn, always worse before it gets better.

"Yeah, well I had a few months to kill before I could call it a life and I thought I better see Europe so I have something to yak about at the retirement home."

"Still playing the young old man I see . . . Jimi?"

"How've you been?"

"Great! We're shooting a movie over here and I'm

in charge of interviewing all the actors . . . American ones! I'll even get to talk to Mickey Rourke!"

"Great, great, so you're pretty busy?"

"There'll be time to chat a bit. I'm staying at my friend William's house in Mayfair near Hyde Park."

I've heard the name William before, some TV whiz kid, invented the game show in London or something groundbreaking like that. Diane's probably fucking him and she, in turn, is getting all the right assignments but I don't know . . . We never get too deep into other relationships. Ours is too tenuous. I'm the mutt in heat begging for some pussy. It's important that I don't give a fuck or at least, that I appear that way—all James Deany, very american.

"Well . . . Yeah . . . You know . . . Whatever . . . I'm here, so call me."

"No, I want to see you RIGHT AWAY. I've got the flat to myself this weekend. I've got to run but I'll call back later and if you're not there I'll leave a meeting place. Is tonight OK?"

"Sure."

"I just need to find out the name of this new place in Soho."

"Sounds good, Diane . . . I'm glad you called."

"Cheers!" and hangs up the phone.

The bottom line is that I'd do anything to get Diane on my arm for a night or a minute or a lifetime. Not that I think it's really possible, because I don't, but these are the kinds of things that keep my dream-state rolling. Diane accepts all the things that make Lindsey gag. Something about the european vibe, they're amused by things the american girls cringe over, like smelly armpits, dirty teeth and greasy hair, bedwetting, no job, no money. It's more of a game to them. Not a Wall Street proposal. I mean I feel kind of out of place when I'm with Diane unless we're on my terms, but that doesn't mean I'm not willing to throw my phallic hat in the ring. She's all the status I ever wanted to pooh-pooh. Some displaced nymphomaniac duchess looking to round out her sexual calendar with a struggling whatever—me. She seems to see some sort of hope in me. Potential. I'm all about the future. I'm a regular forecast. Every success story claims they were once as bleak as me. Eating potato chips, drinking a beer, sitting on the couch, knowing destiny is hiding behind that next Lucky Charms box. Could I be that guy? Could I fill that role? Could I be that snow-white Mandingo? Is it twenty pounds away or is it twenty years away? Or is it just another brick in my outhouse of delusion? I'm on a cloud, a cloud of invisible pillows—my ego. Caught somewhere between love and hate, only ever feeling one or the other. My mood a by-product of my weakness, my genius, my vanity and my lack of true vision. Dime store, all dime store. A tender moment, a moment of total exception. I'm the exception to the rule for a brief moment and I love it. I'm the hero of my own epic. A GIRL LIKES ME AND SHE'S HOT!

Meanwhile, back in the kitchen, the water's boiling up over the rim of the pot. I turn off the flame and divide the scalding water, what's left of it, into two cups. Lost in my *Ben-Hur* sequence, almost all the water's boiled away. I stroll over to the spigot and top off the cups. The water out of the tap is a tad rusty, but it doesn't matter, since I'm making tea. Doobe'll never know the difference. I toss a couple of bags in and watch the water as it takes on more color.

Everyone else is running around the flat, hurrying to get somewhere or another. The air is on the chilly side and I'm hurled on into more "young guy's thoughts." All those, Who am I? What am I? What do I? Where do I? When do I do? Does anybody really know what time it is? kind of thoughts. I don't know. I just don't know! I just want it to be all over! I wanna be somewhere warm looking back on it all, laughing about it. I wanna be rich and slovenly, hiding out on an island, sitting in a bar with dirty khakis telling funny stories about it all. I don't wanna have to GO THROUGH WITH IT ALL. I just want it to be over and I wanna be back on the beach with a drink in my hand, telling whoppers about it all to a Cajun silicon queen who thinks it's all JUST SO CUTE. Right now, I'm knee-deep in the middle of it all and I don't think I like it. It isn't fun. There's too much pressure knowing that I'll have to scrub pots again soon. I wanna be retired and lazy. No ambition. I want that idea or that woman who's gonna change me to come along soon and take care of all this. I want . . . I want . . . I want and I don't have. I don't want the "young guy's thoughts." I want it to be fun. I wanna know the final score of the game so that I can go ahead and start to bet. I want it to be about fucking and I want, I want, I want!

I take hold of the cups and start climbing the steps. Half way up, I spill scorching tea on my right foot. My foot tingles and I jolt, spilling liquid on both my hands. My hands hurt more than my foot now and I got no choice but to forge on ahead up the stairs, half skipping and half crawling. Christ! All I want to do is make a cup of tea for Doobe and I . . . And look what happens! Finally reaching the top, I kick open the door with my unburnt foot. Helms is still sleeping with his fake victorian night-blinders on.

"Wake up, Doober!"

I see a slight quiver of the hand and a toe stretch or two. He's tired. He's been running plates of food by night and being my drinking buddy by day for weeks now. It takes a toll on a guy. It makes morning into afternoon proposition.

"Come on! Wake up, pal! I got some tea I made, almost killed me getting it to ya! We gotta be in good form tonight. That chick Diane's calling me back and we're meeting her tonight in Soho."

"Diane?" I hear from under the pillow.

"You know, that fine royal-type who thinks I'm some kinna thing waiting to happen."

"You are SOME KIND OF THING. A HASSLE."

"Trip to Rio, buddy. Remember that trip to Rio . . ."

"You're getting more mileage outta that far off promise than I thought possible."

"I'm serious. She thinks um like intense like Bobby DeNiro or something. . . ."

"You are . . . *Raging Bull*. You coulda been his double in *Raging Bull*. They coulda used you to focus the lens on . . . You BIG HOUSE."

"Ooch . . . Last time I bring you your cup of morning tea."

"Um just kidding, gimme that tea," pulls off his blinders and reaches for the mug. He takes a sip. I try to suss out by the look on his face whether or not I'm getting on his nerves. It isn't like I add that much to the european skyline. I'm more or less a thorn in his side that needs constant iodine, and that's on my happy days. If I was Doobe, I'd have kicked me out a long time ago. He's still asleep, I figure. The mild disgust on his face, the subtle frown, the squinty eyes are more fatigue than anything I coulda brought about.

"No, um serious though . . . She said she's gonna call back about some marbley kind of new martini bar in Soho."

"Yeah . . . I know the place." Pulls the blinders down over his eyes and flops back down in bed, "Gimme another couple hours . . . Write some HAIKU or something and talk with the girls."

I sit watching TV for a couple hours with the aid of a small chunk of hashish I pirate off the kitchen table. I break small pieces off every twenty minutes and cook them up under glass. No waste, like a crazed scientist. I can feel Diane Rowan on my celestial bicycle path. She is near. Sanctuary is just around the corner. Solace. To be wrapped in the arms of a rich hot british girl is to be OK in the eyes of an ego that's pushed me around the world. To be warm and yet, wrapped in a blanket of ice. Swept away by my fantasy . . . High on top that cliff one more time. Sunbeams shooting off beads of sweat on her shoulders. She's the reason men become losers and villains. Fuck Lindsey! I hate that bitch and all her problems! Even if I did give her a few new ones! Got to get over the curse! The curse of love gone sour! A New Mission. I'm in search of the almighty pink. Diane is the CURE and London's the place! She wants to see me and drink martinis, shaken not fucking stirred!

Pulp 28

"Boys, boys, boys . . . Little american boys drinking man's drinks!" Miss Diane gives me a decent hug. I say "decent," which is like getting a blow job from an american girl. The british are cold, so cold that physical contact in public is almost indecent.

"How ya doin', Diane . . . How ya been?" I hug her back, weighing the response, searching the embrace for some sign of where I stand on the "guys I wanna fuck" list.

"This is my buddy, Doobe, I've been tellin' you about."

"Hi Diane. It's a pleasure . . . Jimi's told me a lot about you as well."

"Well, cheers to you, Dink! Jimi said that you were just so sweet and wasn't he JUST so right!"

"It's Doobe, Diane. D-O-O-B-E . . . DOOBE."

"Well I'm sorry Doobe," she flutters, "I meant no harm!" and sits down.

A delicate hand through her hair and she orders a glass of chablis. Christ, I could just LOOK at the bitch. The kind of chick that you look at even when they're with huge muscle-butt steroid guys because it just doesn't matter. It's out of your hands! You just look at them! They strike . . . They appear . . . They vanish . . . And there's nothing left to do but loop your mule in memory of them. They stop you in the middle of a sentence. You look at them right in front of the fat bitch sitting next to you. Diane becomes the face on all your average-looking fucks. The kind of woman you think you're willing to pay the price for. Class . . . A blue french miniskirted suit . . . Black leather go-go boots . . . Dirty-blond hair with still a bit of sun on her pale freckly skin. It's hard for me to believe I boned this woman! No. . . . She isn't a woman . . . She's a young lady. I wanna lean over and tell this young thing, this vision, this 900 number sound-alike look-doll, this stroke of luck that she can be my adultress forever. I want to lean over and tell this 3-D fantasy that she can just go ahead and destroy any relationship I'm ever gonna have. I don't wanna even TRY to be her steady man. Too many social events. I just wanna be that token vagabond fuck. She takes a sip of wine and I'm sure the way she drinks that wine . . . The way it dances across her tongue and the way she follows it with that magnificent cashmere lick of the lips and finally, that smile . . . I'm sure that's just the way Grace Kelly used to do it, and Grace Kelly was the most beautiful woman ever. I mean I respect Cary Grant solely for the fact that I once saw him slap Grace Kelly, regardless of how many young nubile boys he chased around his house in maids' outfits. She's so prim and proper and yet I'll bet she's never stayed up a single night worrying about her moral code. Morals are for the masses. I worry about morals! I try to have morals because somewhere along the line I was tricked into thinking that it fucking mattered! Like there's a right way to do things! It's all just a dirty little spin-the-bottle game to Diane.

We spend the better part of the afternoon drinking at the bar. The martinis flow endlessly like they're being pissed out of little cupid-statue-fountains. I snort down half a dozen before I get up to take my first leak. I do a lot of listening, nodding my head, and dreaming. Diane and Doobe do a lot of yakking. I soak it ALL in, wondering if I'll get a chance to hole up, like a pair of deviant Tinker toys, with the duchess in sugar-boy William's flat near Hyde Park. I make eye contact. I give a slurry smile and get a little play—a couple of brief pauses in her head as it turns past me and that's enough for me. Enough to make me think good thoughts, my only hurdle being the viral uproar I got south of the navel. Time has been oh so cruel. My rod's bloomed, looking like a twisted bouquet of O'Keeffe lilies from the FTD of hell, leaving me highly contagious. You might catch it standing downwind of me in the johns. I've never told Diane that I got the herpes but I figure as long as I'm honest about it, she'll be cool. She's a big girl. I just gotta be honest! In the meantime, I gotta sneak out the door like I'm going to the head and score a pack of King James version Trojans to wrap my piece in. I got a lucky feeling tonight and I wanna have protection with me as long as my groin still looks like bad pop art.

Doobe and Diane are going on about some political shit and I make like I'm going to the bathroom, turn a quick hard left and scoot out the door. I spot a variety store across the street and cop a trusty three-pack at the counter. Still embarrassed after all these years, I buy a candy bar. I sneak back across the street and duck in next to the two chatterboxes at the bar.

Another couple rounds and a whole lotta laughs later, Diane's grabbing me.

"Dizzy, I'm taking your friend with me! Is that OK? I've got to talk to him a little bit alone but you're very nice too! We just haven't seen each other for awhile!"

"That's OK with me . . . I could use a night alone. I need to do some laundry I think," and he waves. I'm an object.

"Don't worry, you'll get him back!" and drags me away.

Boy Wonder Willi's flat is a sick sort of turn-of-the-century swanky Gatsby pad, nestled in the heart of Mayfair, which I guess is as good as it gets in Fog Town. The place's got high, high ceilings and a spiral staircase built only for the likes of Vivien Leigh, big billowy curtains and all the things that a place like this is supposed to have inside of it. I'm peeking around every corner, waiting for David Niven to come out and hand me a glass of sherry. Candlelight. Candles going everywhere, like a Buddhist temple. It's beyond wealth! Sets of knights' armor, family crests, the works.

Diane pulls me right up the stairs into the wall-to-wall velvet master bedroom and I figure it's as good a time as any to let the evil cat out of the bag.

"Diane, I gotta tell ya something . . . I got the herpes and I'm having an outbreak . . . I don't want you to get it, so we gotta be really careful."

"HERPES . . . " she cries. "OH YOU MUST BE JOKING, REALLY . . . YOU GOT THE HERPES!

WHY I CAN'T EVEN BELIEVE THAT . . . HER-PES! AND YOU THINK I'M GOING TO SLEEP WITH YOU . . . HERPES! YOU MUST BE OUT OF YOUR MIND . . . HERPES!"

Everytime she says the word, I see a giant black crow cawing and shaming me with a treacherous beak. My heart is off to the races, screaming up at me, telling me to find a ledge and jump. I look at her with that smirking superior mug, sitting perfect while I nurse my case of sexual chicken pox. Her eyes grow strange, distant. She's pulling away. The woman that I thought was my second biggest fan, my believer, turns on me, looks at me like I'm Rock Hudson's kid brother.

"Look . . . I chose to be honest with you . . . and you start to make fun of me?"

"OH, OK THERE . . . MISTER HERPES SLEAZE MAN! MISTER AMERICAN GIGOLO HERPES SLEAZE MAN!" She laughs.

I can't believe it, my biggest nightmare come true. First, I get the herpes from some lying rich girl I sleep with, because I find out she's from a famous family and I'm trying to smooch my way up through the social-economic ranks. And now . . . I'm being condemned by this Limey countess. I'm indignant!

"Look Miss Jet-Set Bitch . . . If you don't wanna sleep with me tonight that's one thing. But don't lay THIS shit on me! I didn't HAVE to be honest with you in the first place, you superior little dollop!"

I pull away from her wicked grinning face. I can't even look at her anymore, that sadistic laughing face.

I stumble back and turn towards the window, the freedom. I can't stand this fucking bitch . . . It's over!

"Poor Jimi-boy . . . His little herpes sores have him just all in an uproar!" she sings with mock pity. I'm back on the playground being taunted. Childhood Flashback Nightmare. Thank god, I never wet the bed around this one! I got no other choice, I'm in hell. I got no other choice but to reach for the nearest satin pillow and smack the woman. Give her a good wallop! Give her something to choke on! Shut her up with some of India's finest fabric. I give her a good one from over the top of my head . . . BAMMM! It woulda made my brutish sister proud back in the old days, and she goes down. I regain my form and charge at her, ready to give her a few finishing POWS when our eyes meet and I freeze. The look in her eye stops me. I see the mistake.

"Jimi," she screams, "what've you lost your fucking mind! I was kidding!"

"What?"

"Almost all you americans have the herpes. I worked on one of William's documentaries about it! I was just bloody kidding! I don't care!"

"Christ . . . Diane . . . I mean you sure fucking had your fun with THAT joke!"

Straightening out her hair, her face flushed, ". . . But that other stuff . . . About the Jet-Set Bitch and whatnot . . . Why did you say that? That's a different matter entirely."

Paradise is over. I've played out my last trump card . . . Whatever that means. Once again, I've revealed myself for the misguided power tool that I am. For like an hour, I smooth and I lie. I even outright beg for several long stints but nothing can take away the smelly dead fishes of words that I puked out onto the floor.

"I mean . . . I guess I gotta say that the herpes thing is like my Achilles' fucking heel and . . . I just didn't catch your whole british comedic approach thing. I thought you meant it. You caught me way off guard."

"I understand, Jimi . . . But why did you call me names and say things like I'm some kind of monied flooze? I've never been like that with you."

"You haven't . . . I don't know . . . It was just what came out in the rage . . . I didn't really mean it," I plead.

Probably out of exhaustion, she lets up. We're both sobered up by now, and back down on the planet from our martini-induced tirade. I'd have to say that my approach on this very evening will always be something that I consider to be a HUGE MISTAKE.

I blew it. Diane loved me because I got this kind of high-tech pseudo-romantic sort of devil-may-care attitude, and now it's over. My emotions' not being in sync with my little, intense, rambling guy kind of vagabond chooch rebel rap, and it's over. I've become just another neurotic loser with a flair for the secondhand leathery facade. Looking for a piece of pussy pie and reading it all wrong. Who knows, maybe it added to the intrigue? I don't know anything anymore. Women are more of a know anything anymore. Women are more of a mystery to me than world hunger.

I go for broke. I grab Diane and plant one on her roughly, jamming my tongue between her struggling lips. She pulls away at first but I stay right with her, and she finally settles down at the end of my tongue. Her lips are soft and warm like fruity roasted marshmallows. I wanna bite them . . . And I do. Her tongue tastes of white wine. I suck on it. I nibble on the fleshy rinds of her lips. She squirms, still fighting ever so slightly, but I know I'm in for a run on the bush. I can get it, it's all about just waiting 'til the time is ripe. She wants me, she's trembling against me like a scared puppy that doesn't want to be kicked again but stays . . . For the same brand of loving and affection. I look past her out the window. I count the dull yellow lamps along the street and all the other row houses stacked along the other side of the street. Red Brick Wombs in the Middle of the Chaos. I feel comfortable in this guy, William's flat. It makes me wanna be rich . . . And powerful.

"I like this house, Diane . . . I like this world. It makes me wanna be famous."

"There aren't any famous people here . . . These people are REALLY rich. It's a different world. There's too much at stake."

I don't really know what she means, but with her hand down along the shaft of my penis, she's got my complete and utter attention. Anything is OK, I'm just a kid from Pittsburgh about to be knee-deep into some of the finest british LASS I've ever known or seen. I haven't worked in a month or two . . . My hair looks OK . . . Yeah . . . I know exactly what she means . . . I think . . . I just can't quite remember what the hell she said or what we were talking about . . . Oh yeah . . . Money . . . I'm lost in a fantasy . . . I'm skipping down the streets of my dreams . . . The dialogue is unimportant . . . The words just a clever little veil . . . A decoy away from . . . The thoughts . . . And the feelings . . . That leave us soaked in sweat . . . And crying . . . The real shit goes like . . . In a fucking song or something . . . It's not sublime . . . Like . . . I rip her clothes off with no regard whatsoever for high fashion . . . I see her pussy and I go right for it . . . It's so blond that it looks almost hairless in the soft light . . . Smooth and fresh . . . Young . . . I don't fumble . . . I'm right there . . . Right on it in no time . . . I have my finger up there . . . I have my tongue up there . . . It isn't two minutes before I have my tongue so far up her little round behind that I got no choice but to make funny little obscene snorting noises . . . It's beautiful . . . I'm comfortable in this neighborhood . . . I want to lick every part of this girl . . . I suck on her toes . . . I lick her armpits . . . Jesus . . . I can't even talk anymore . . . That pussy with its pink folds and its uptown juices . . . NOTHING MATTERS . . . I lap . . . I suck . . . I flick . . . I push . . . I want to absorb her . . . Engulf her with my tongue . . . Until finally she comes . . . Trembling . . . And shaking . . . For long enough that I can flip her over and work on her tight little sphincter . . . She's mine if only for a few seconds . . . She can be anyone's . . . She can be her own . . . I don't care . . . It doesn't matter . . . That's all politics . . . And bullshit . . . And power . . . And this is sex . . . I'm a loser . . . I'm a winner . . . I'm afraid . . . I'm a fraud . . . It's all words . . . It's all BULLSHIT!

I continue to nibble on her clit while I fumble through my pockets looking for those damn hiding rubbers, never seem to be in the same pocket I put them in. It's hard to keep up the intensity but I do my best. Diane's pussy juice is all over my face. I feel like the floor of a Good Humor truck on the hottest day in July. It's frustrating but I finally manage to roll the latex sock down the length of my rig. I slither my way back to her wanting mouth with soft kisses . . . Allowing . . . Offering my mouth full of her. Her pussy is now wide open and fully juiced and I begin to ease my cellophaned member down deep. It's warm even with the raingear on. I feel at home. I wanna cry. I never want to leave. It's so rare I feel safe. Like I'm gonna spend the rest of my life sitting around waiting in cold empty bus stations in towns like Denver and Santa Fe and Washington . . . Always waiting to leave . . . Always feeling like it's time to go. Instead of curling up deep in warm motherpussy. I stroke long . . . Gentle and soft . . . I hope my rubber doesn't break and give her my little curse . . . I kiss her . . . I love her but I can't tell her . . . I pray I don't infect her . . . I turn my head away . . . I have to look around her . . . She'll know I care too much . . . I hope I don't ruin her . . . I hope I don't ruin this . . . Please, Mr. Rubber, don't burst . . . I'm floating . . . I'm free . . . Don't let this thing end . . . I love this feeling . . . Can't give her my burden . . . And I come . . . Slowly and painfully . . . With a groan from my Inner never-never land . . . From somewhere inside of me that I can't get to alone . . . I arch my back and close my eyes . . . And go black for the release . . . I collapse into a sweating ball on top of her . . . Clinging to her . . . A clown warming a cave, born for a prince.

PULP 29

Lying in bed with sleeping arms around me, I remember sitting in a chair in a house surrounded by cats. Eight or nine of the furry little aloof fuckers looking up at me, sniffing me. I love the house. It's the Good Witch's house and I love cats because the Good Witch taught me to love cats. Cats are like people with guts. Most people don't like cats because they want them to be like sappy dogs yearning for affection, wanting to be owned. The dogs are fine. It's the people. Cats are loners, cool loners who just drop in now and then and say, "Hello," and maybe grab a quick bite to eat. The Good Witch told me that you always have to keep a few spares around the house because cats tend to die untimely deaths. There are a lot of Cat Killers out there. I mighta been a Cat Killer but I met the Good Witch. I'm not listening to the cats though, I'm listening to Lindsey.

"Jimi, I just don't feel that good about myself right now. It isn't you. I don't know . . . I guess I feel kind of dirty or something."

Yeah, I know that feeling . . . I've had it for a coupla years. It gets a little better but it never goes away. Sometimes it gets worse. A slowing burning. Fucking. It's fucking that caused all this. Desire can make a lot of shitty things happen, it seems.

". . . I just need to get back to Boston . . . And then I think things'll get better."

"Away from me?"

"No . . . Not 'away from you' really . . . I just need some time . . . Life sorta stops out here on the island . . . You know?"

"That's why I like it."

"I mean I do too . . . It's just, I need to do a few things first. I need some time, Jimi."

Why don't I have the balls to look her in the eye and say, "Look Lindsey . . . I know this thing's doomed so let's not even worry about it anymore. It's over so let's shake hands and fucking walk our separate ways!" No . . . Of course I can't do that! I have to stay in the misery and plead for Lindsey to linger on with me for as long as we can take it. The worst part is that I'll wade through this word-game shit for hours, knowing damn well

I'm just trying to get my dick in her ONE MORE TIME. That's the worst part! Even at my lowest moments, I'm still thinking "What's in it for me?" At my age, lust is stronger than love. I want some more of that shit! It's my self-duty to convince Lindsey that the only cure for the pain and confusion is a good old-fashioned coming. The Good Witch and the Cats understand. Oh sweet Lindsey . . . Just another pin in the balloon of life. I mean WHO ever felt all that good about life to begin with?

I get up out of bed and tiptoe my way down to the kitchen. I peek into the fridge . . . BINGO . . . A stray chilly beer just waiting to nurse Jimi's aching liver. I take a long, suffocating slurp and look out the window. It's late at night. I don't know the time, but late enough that I feel some peace. I love the night. There's nothing to prove at night, as long as the imagination doesn't run wild in the wrong direction. Diane's sound asleep. Her breathing whispers down through the foyer, serene, unscathed by the monster of worry, or doubt. One last look at the dick. Yep, sores abloom. Another sip of beer . . . And another . . . And another . . . And the street . . . And all the yellow lamps . . . And all the figures off in the distance . . . And another . . . And another . . . All the people . . . All the places . . . And all the tears . . . And all the laughter . . . And all of Mister Rogers' Neighborhood . . . It isn't real . . . This is a fantasy . . . None of this is real . . . And another sip of beer . . . Success is just a fool's word for survival.

Pulp30

"It's just so fuckin' odd. She called you DOOGE when I talked to her."

"Whatever . . . The Groucho Club'll be fun no matter what she calls me."

"It sounds cool. Her boy 'Willi' is in town . . . Says he's 'dying to meet me' . . . I'll bet."

"As long as Willi's buying, we're dying to meet him too, Jimi."

We got a couple hours before we go to the stuffy London club. Doobe and I sit down in Gilbert and Sullivan and drink whiskey—beautiful sour mash by the bucket, not shitty ale, GOOD WHISKEY. Helms and I don't trust ourselves, so we tell our Gracelandish barkeep pal to keep us abreast of the time. Early evening in Leicester Square, with all the workaday frenzy. My favorite TV show, and the butterflies are coming in my stomach. The Beginning of Night. The hum . . . The pulse . . . The buzz . . . Call it whatever you fucking want, the shit is real. I remember running up my street on Friday nights when I was younger, running up to meet my friends in the woods to smoke weed out of our latest "Monster Bong," to drink that warm Iron City keg, to get drunk enough to go meet girls and act tough. It meant everything to me.

Diane said the Groucho Club is some heavy-duty club where all the London writers hang out and talk about their next "Movie of the Week" assignment or "that latest piece on the new cafe," the one "all the Harleys park in front of." Talk about who's gonna play the psycho-mother and what guy they want to play the daughter-molesting dad. Heavy stuff . . . Politics . . . And the *New Yorker* . . . I got one thing on my mind . . . FREE DRINKS.

First, there's the standard drunken directional confusion, and then Helms gets us on the right path to the club. The Groucho is inside a modest brick building, the only giveaway being a tux-clad butthead doorman standing his ground in front of a maroon door under a lone lamp. We stand out front in the street, not quite sure what comes next. A perfect time for us to start smoking Lucky Strikes. We opt to shuffle our feet and act relaxed, practicing our favorite movie-star walks, until Diane pops her dirty-blond head out the front door and spots us.

"Jimi Banks and his loyal cohort . . . Mr. Helms," she giggles.

Everytime I see the girl she looks hotter. Tonight's no different. She's decked out in some scant bell-bottomed Edie Sedgwick outfit. Rich chicks . . . Even their sweat looks like something that should be served with an olive.

"Ms. Rowan," I follow suit.

"Diane, you DO look good tonight, dear!" Doobe slurs and we're busted. Here it comes.

"You're drunk aren't you? . . . Look at the both of you!"

Judging by the sharp stare and the haughty tone, in Diane's mind, we've picked the wrong night to drink bourbon all day.

"Well . . . I guess it's too late now, isn't it?"

Diane spins around and we follow her in, smirking past the constipated-looking Hercules at the door and up a flight of stairs. At the top of the stairs is a swinging double door. I can hear all the "Oh REEEEEEEEAAALLLLLYYYYY" voices bouncing around inside the club as we hit the doors. I lean over to Doobe and whisper, "I hear more high-winded laughing in there than in a fucking hyena convention." He breaks out with a barleycorned guffaw and Diane turns, "OK boys . . . We're here," as if the house band's about to go into our opening number, and swings open the door.

Pulp 31

The Groucho Club is everything F. Scott Fitzgerald would've needed it to be. High crystal chandeliers, violins playing, champagne glasses being ching-chinged and people, all pasty pale and very british, laughing that laugh. Laughing that laugh that echoes and makes me wince. Laughing that laugh that comes from up high, never low . . . Then there's William.

Whenever I'm with a girl who's hanging out with another guy, I get that same mental picture of him. Tall, clean-cut, plastic hair, TV-actor smile. The kind of guy who irons his blue jeans and pairs his socks and invites his women camping and like, snowboarding—all the things that he just really "grooves on." I see Willi-boy and once again, my imagination has foiled my ass. Willi's about 5'4" with a semi-bald head, nothing but sidewalls and two regulation DAISY-brand BBs for eyes. He's got a body that would look good over a hanger—wire hanger, not wood.

"Jimi, this is William."

"Pleasure," he says and drops out a feathery paw for me to examine. I take the thing in my hand. I've held onto firmer soaked toilet paper before. The kind of hand that's never thrown a baseball or properly tickled a clitoris. Our eyes meet, and we both shudder from that same "oh my god, you fucked her too" feeling. It runs up and down our arms while we shake.

"This is my buddy, Doobe Helms."

"Oh . . . The one with the funny name . . . I'm William."

"How Willi . . . How ya doin'? Diane tells us you're a real kingfish in these parts," Doobe says in his best Appalachian drawl. I want to lean over and kiss Doobe for such poignant icebreaking. Diane, etiquette metronome that she is, clears her throat and beckons the waiter.

"Scotch, the best you've got . . . A pair of them," I call with a certain Doobe-goaded cockiness. I don't know how long the civility will last, so I figure I should order the good stuff right outta the shoot.

"So Jimi . . . Diane tells me you're traveling through Europe."

"Yeah . . . That's about it . . . America's getting to be a bit MUCH for me."

"What is it . . . Exactly . . . That you do?"

"Nothing . . . Really . . . Exactly."

"How interesting."

"I guess . . ." taking a long swig of scotch. Doobe and Diane are back into one of their friendly raps across the table. It looks like it's me and Willi-boy doing the sophisticated "get to know you" convo.

"Do you like our city?"

"Yeah . . . I mean . . . It's not like I've worked or anything since I got here . . . So of course it seems GREAT."

I take another gulp of scotch. I'm beginning to hate this guy, William. He's like a linen version of all the assholes I went to college with. Diane and Doobe are chatting away still, and I'm stuck at this end of the table, playing 40 QUESTIONS WITH TV EXEC MAN for free booze.

"How do your parents feel about the life you lead?"

"Well actually, Willi, I think that as long as I stay

out of jail . . . They just sort of stay quietly disappointed."

"What do you tell them you want to do?"

"I guess be an actor mostly . . . I tell them I yearn for the stage . . . Oh yeah . . . And lately I've been telling them that I wanna be a rock star. How 'bout you? What do you do?"

"I create TV shows."

"Now there's a field that I could take home with me and throw out on the Christmas table."

"Excuse me?"

"What I mean is, that's the kind of thing Moms just love to hear . . . I mean as long as you're good at it, I guess . . . You know . . . Doing your part to keep the network ball rolling and everything."

"My Mum's dead."

"You know . . . Isn't it always that way."

I'm through with this one. I don't even care what the guy thinks. I'm not talking any longer. I figure the best thing to do is to just start looking around the room, just act really distracted and I can escape from this pinstriped diatribe. There are so many fine women in the room—all tall bitches. I've never been somewhere where Diane looked almost below average. But in this room, she's borderline spinster. Every time I turn my head, I get the feeling I'm drowning on the *Vogue* cutting-room floor. So tall! I figure there must be a little wooden clown in the ladies room that all the women have to be taller than, like next to the roller-coaster rides back home. Most of the women are with short goofy-looking guys, too. Some kind of justice bestowed on all the dweebs of the world, that they grow up to lasso a few tall bitches. Sweet revenge for all the years of being picked last in the kickball draft at recess.

Diane ends up catching a nice little gin buzz, bless her soul, and takes control of the table, keeping us all laughing and light. She's the link. It's a title she holds with relish, I'm sure. Doobe's eyes have begun to take on the mist of lechery I can't help but notice. I think his little *tête-à-têtes* with Diane have sprung a rod in his slacks as well. She has us all under her spell.

The rounds of scotch never stop coming. I'm almost starting to like Willi. Every drop of scotch that tickles his throat jars loose another standard kind of, "You guys live the life . . . Bumming around . . . I'm trapped in my world . . . I wanna take up the travelers' life." It's a pretty common ailment amongst the ridiculously established; they tend to wax nostalgic about that one month when they didn't get a haircut and ate a handful of mushrooms.

"When I was in university . . . They called me 'Wild Willi' 'cause on the weekends I became a bloody beast. I miss those feelings. I miss that reputation, heehee."

"I'll bet ya do, Willi . . . Ya seem to have a little bit of a madman in you." Anything to keep the tab soaring. These guys love it when you tell 'em that they really should be poets and thieves. That they have the goods to go underground.

"Oh boys . . . Let's go dancing now. I'm absolutely DYING to dance at the WAG!"

We all agree, and get up to leave. Willi's left to handle the tab, and Doobe and I make for the door. I'm walking alongside Doobe, slaloming After Six wear, when my eyes zoom in on what appears to be a cart, filled with the most lavish desserts my Dairy Queen nigger-rich eyes have ever beheld. Forget about it! Unparalleled! Desserts like I've only dreamed of! And I hadn't really eaten much of anything in a coupla days. Life is only SO beautiful when you're frying up spuds three times a day! Oh lord. Oh my, oh my . . . To savor that sugar on my palate if only but for a second . . . Better than a night out with Ann-Margret and Ursula Andress mainlining oyster oil . . . I can taste it . . . I want it . . . I can't believe I didn't squeeze a meal out of Willi, what was I thinking? . . . It woulda gone so well with that top-shelf scotch . . . There's tarte Tatin I'd murder for . . . Oh my . . . All flat and luscious with scalloped apples floating in pools of goo . . . The sugar gleaming off the meaty fruit . . . The juice running off over the crust rim . . . Little whipped cream flowerettes poised on top . . . Jewels on the crown . . . Chocolate cake so rich and thick . . . Chunks . . . Floating across the tray . . . Stray cocoa icebergs of joy . . . Nuts on top the size of prewar brick . . . I see a cheesecake as big as a mattress . . . Held hostage under swollen blueberries and strawberries . . . Yelling to me . . . Jimi . . . It's worth the gamble . . . Begging to be devoured . . . Pudding in baby-poolish bowls . . . It isn't fair . . . I want it . . . And I'm walking away meekly . . . Some rich jerk's gonna leave half of it on his plate . . . It just isn't fair . . . I want it.

"Jump on it, Jimi . . . It's yours, pal . . . I got ya covered!"

What I don't realize is that Doobe's been laughing at me the whole time, watching my eyes drool, and he knows what I want. He can feel my granulated yearning.

"Do you think I can get away with it?"

"I KNOW you can!" Doobe says it, and I wanna hear it, so it must be true! I want it! I know I can do it, he's right! I just gotta make a clean sweep of it, that's all! It would be easier if I could just shrink and stay for a day, but I can't, I gotta go for it now!

"Come on, now! Get on it!"

My heart speeds up and I look around one last time. No one cares. All these people are having fun. They don't care if I take a few for the road. It looks good . . . I can do it . . . One quick swoop of the hand catches a chunk of goo from off the cheesecake and I jam it into my pocket . . . I can't leave the mangled remnants down on the cart and I go back down once again . . . Jam into the squishy pocket and give the culprit fingers a quick licking to hide the evidence . . . I look up at the crowd . . . All heads are pointed at me . . . I remember the EF Hutton commercials of my youth . . . It would be hard to get as much attention as I'm getting without brandishing a .357 wildly in the air . . . The blank faces indicate it wasn't a very good grab . . . I look back at the tray . . . It's quite clear I destroyed the better part of almost EVERY dessert on the cart . . . In my mind . . . I blame it on the scotch.

"You got it, buddy! Don't let their looks deceive you! You got it good!"

We get outside and Doobe gives me a bittersweet patting on the back.

"Took a lotta guts in there, Jimi . . . I'm prouda ya!"

We look back inside to see a beet-faced William, talking to the maître d', peeling bills off a huge roll, all under a shadowing Diane trying desperately to salvage some face. I look back, shrug, hand some cheese goo to Doobe, and we both stuff our mouths. It's clear to me . . . Someone's always watching.

Pulp 32

The WAG reminds me of too many roller-skating rinks I hung out in as a delinquent tyke. Old chipped red wood, that stale smell, scratchy music, old posters suggesting that THIS had once been a happening place. I can't figure out why we're here.

It's so un-Diane. Either she's trying to hide out while she's with a couple losers like us, or maybe she lost a cherry here and always comes home. It's below a coffee shop that's only open when the club isn't—a gimmick. Anyways, little Willi's still ticked despite my snickering apologies. He's turned his focus completely on Diane. It's US and THEM. Diane's taken on the beauty that only rears its ugly head in the terminal stages of a binge. Even if she were plain, she'd look ravishing. I look at her while she dances with Willi. Legs up to her ears, dancing more goofy than sexy, with Willi, that little tuba-eared fuck.

To see me losing once again . . . I love her . . . I know that I do . . . Vulgar . . . My actions . . . My mind . . . All vulgar . . . Something about a jar of Vaseline . . . A bullwhip . . . A stack of old comics . . . She's my girl. Doobe's busy dancing with some local tarts—bad makeup, the gap-tooth, the whole bit. I wanna dance with Diane but my legs are frozen. I wanna run over to her and tell her that I love her. I wanna be in a fifties movie with a butthead pal named Bronco who could start a fight and clear the bar, and I can run away with Diane. I want everyone to stay in my little world . . . But they're leaving me . . . I want Diane . . . I wanna kiss again . . . I'm teeming . . . I have to act . . . I need a plan . . . OH FUCK IT . . . I run out onto the dance floor . . . Hands and arms flail at me.

"Diane . . . I love you . . . I can't watch you dance

with this geek anymore . . . Come back to America with me . . . I do . . . I really love you!"

I might as well have pulled down my pants and pissed all over the dance floor. Diane starts to laugh.

"Jimi . . . You must be KIDDING . . . I'm sorry for all of this, William."

Red seas will part and relationships will all close, as did the crowd around Diane and Willi. She won't look at me. I know this. I know that whatever it was, it's over. I never understood it. I wouldn't even care, if I had just known for a second what it was. I don't want it back. I know I can't have it. I just wanna know what it ever even was. I stand out on the dance floor for as long as I can, trying not to feel like I'm reacting to Diane, and then I go back to my beer. I look for Diane ten minutes later and she's gone. Doobe's dancing with the tarts and I hit him up for money for another beer. Watch the crowd, all dance without rhythm, but having a good time. I muster a smile.

"This'll all be so fucking funny in ten years," I tell myself. "I'll look back and maybe she will too."

Another sip and Doobe finishes dancing and joins me.

"What happened to Diane and Waldo?"

"They said they had to go . . . Something about getting up for work."

"That guy was a fucking dweeb."

"He was alright, Doobe . . . Actually . . . I think he was just Diane's type."

"Yeah . . . I guess you're right . . . He was OK."

Pulp33

Daylight creeps into the room with feet of lead. My eyes, or rather, the sockets that once housed my eyes, burn in welcome. Instinct thrusts my hand into my pants and comes up barren. NO WALLET. There's no reason for confusion, I'M IN A BIND. Things were bleak in the past, but time has been good to the ugliness, and things have gotten bleaker. The hangover is a nice aside. If I was at all spiritual, now would be the time to walk into the ocean with flowers in my hand. Instead, I walk downstairs to hunt for stray hashish crumbs and a hot cup of tea. The pain born in my eye sockets is welting my toes now—COMPLETE COVERAGE.

"It's all been a huge mistake . . . Things've managed to get worse." It's all kind of GROOVY with a polluted head but the pillow cushions of the comfort zone are wearing thin now. Nothing left but fucking reality. BUTT-FUCKING REALITY.

A stroll to the bathroom for a leak. I look into the mirror and spy a rancid melon glaring me down. Fuck the eyes being the window into the soul, my seething cheeks alone are reason enough to call for

an exorcism. I thought I left all my troubles behind in America. Wasn't I the same guy who wanted to lose it all? Who wanted to cleanse? To have nothing to lose? Fuck . . . That shit sounds good until the music stops and the lights go up! This is it . . . THE END OF MY LINE. I'm waiting for Doobe to wake me up and kick me out into the streets! Homeless in London, that would be lower, yeah, that would definitely be lower. This shit is bad. I can't even find my toothbrush. Being at that point in life where people you know say things with a wince like, "Yeah . . . Things haven't worked out too well for Jimi . . . He's havin' a tough time of it . . . Tough goin' kiddo." You've laughed at it in the movies and now . . . IT'S MY LIFE. It's all someone else's funny story in a bar, that's it. It's not my life! This is someone else's bad joke! I'm not a part of this! How long do I have to be somebody else's tragedy? Five years? Ten? Fifty? A lifetime? That's a long time to come up short! I close the bathroom door and sit down with my face . . . and the dreaded mirror.

I cry. It begins as an exercise and ends as a twisted ballet. Writhing on the floor, bleeding a sad clown face. I can't remember how long it's been since I cried. I cry for Ray . . . I cry for Lindsey . . . I cry for my mom . . . I cry for the old man . . . For Diane . . . For Doobe . . . For London . . . I cry for rain . . . I cry for summers that I had when I was little . . . I cry for memories . . . For the world . . . For MY world . . . I cry and I cry and I bury my face in my hands . . . Grinding my fists into my eyes . . . I'm ashamed . . . Ashamed because I cry like a baby . . . Because I don't know . . . Because I don't have any answers . . . Because I don't have any money . . . Because I'm afraid . . . I cry for me . . . Most of all . . . I CRY FOR ME. . . .

Pulp 34

For two days, I sit around the house and drink whatever I can find short of Sterno. Start off the day with a double NyQuil on the rocks. The pattern is set. Wake up, smoke hashish with the girls, they leave and I get on the booze-full train of sorrow and hiding. By noon every day, I get the pen out and I'm trying to write letters to Lindsey. It's either that or call Diane, and I don't particularly want to hear what anyone else has to say. I start out every time with lots of poetic bullshit, all passionate and violiny and by the second paragraph, my hand's making lines across the page—shut down. Nothing to do but drink more and pray for 80-proof rain. Finally, the booze runs out and I decide to take a walk.

The sun's gone down and I can see the air in front of me. I walk for an hour before I even realize that I'm walking. I walk and I walk. I start to wake up early in the morning and I take walks through all the neighborhoods. I take the tube across town and I walk. Get up, fry potatoes, drink a pot of tea and walk. Looking, smelling, thinking, and dreaming. I walk until it gets dark, and then I catch a train and go home and eat a few more potatoes. The potatoes fill me up but I'm still always hungry. I watch the traffic, and the lights, and the people, and the trees, until I'm so hungry that everything begins to vibrate. At that point, I'm just coasting through a Cézanne painting, everything jagged and vibrating, jumping into my fourth dimension. I begin to lose weight and all the boys start taking notice. Jeans hanging off my hips and all those fickle boys loving me. I'm bony. I got cheekbones! No longer the suave stepson of the Elephant Man.

I hit a piazza one day in the middle of town and I get a load of this statue. The usual—tall, stoic, uniform, big chin, the works . . . When a slight detail catches my eye . . . ONE ARM. The motherfucker's got one arm! Turns out, as I skim the plaque at his boot, that it's Admiral Nelson. Apparently this guy beat the whole Spanish Armada with not only one arm . . . BUT ONE EYE! Talk about making me feel like a weasel! I got the herpes and my buddy offed himself and I'm broke . . . This guy, Nelson, beat a whole fleet of the world's baddest ships with like rowboats and cap guns. It's all I can do not to skip home followed by a band of admiring Liberace look-alikes. I'm happy this motherfucker beat the odds. It gives me hope. Hope and an idea—A DIME STORE KIND OF BRAINSTORM.

Pulp35

JIMI IS CALLING FROM LONDON . . . WILL YOU ACCEPT THE CHARGES?

"Yes . . . I'll accept the charges."

"Unc?"

"Jimi?"

"Hey . . . How ya doin'?"

"Good, Jimi . . . I think the question is . . . How are you doin'?"

"Actually . . . Somethin' went down."

"What a surprise."

"I lost my wallet with all my money."

"And your passport?"

"No, I didn't have my passport with me."

"Where'd you lose it?"

"You know? . . . I'm not quite sure. It's all a little hazy that night."

"So now you need money?"

"I do, Unc."

"You know you coulda come up with a better one if you were going to call me collect from London and ask me for dough."

"The weirdest thing is that it's actually true . . . I swear, Unc."

"Yeah, well . . . I'll drop you some cash at Western Union . . . It oughta be there by tomorrow since it's already so late in London."

"Unc . . . I owe you one."

"No . . . If you owed me ONE . . . Then you'd owe me A COUPLE . . . But you don't owe me anything . . . I gotta go to work . . . I'll see you later."

I've never been a big fan of holidays with the family or even THE FAMILY PERIOD . . . But times like this make it GOOD to have a group of people who feel at least MILDLY obligated to give a fuck! It's the little victories, the small triumphs that keep the Kool-Aid Smile on my face.

PvlP36

Memories are a big hassle. They weigh more than any pile of gravel I ever shoveled. I'm a slave to my past . . . I'm a slave to the pussy . . . I'm a slave to the car . . . The land . . . The desire to be something I'm not . . . I'm a slave to everything that weighs.

Lying in bed with a pocket full of someone else's money, desperately needing a new pair of socks. PARIS. What two-bit dreamer didn't go there and talk about how rude the waiters were? A song sung a million times by ten million different mooks like me.

It all started with a phone call from Jane, Ray's last girlfriend, to Doobe, asking us to come see her. It's a long way from the vacation hot spot of my youth—WILDWOOD, NEW JERSEY. Personally, I'm not all that keen on seeing the chick, but Doobe thinks it'll be nice, so we're doing it. I got a friend of a friend over there by the name of Harry Clements, who I figure I'll look up when I get there.

I'll go. I'm tired of London and I'm starting to catch up with myself here. Time for a new town. It's always better when I'm coming or going, just watching it all pass by through the window.

Jackson Pollock coulda painted the sky, I think, as I turn over and look for another pillow. I'm not really one to go on about nature and its power, but I gotta cop to the fact that there are moments when I am all but brought to my knees by Big Mamma. Something about leaving makes me feel relaxed. I watch the sky, all the shades of blue and black splattered and I think about Paris and I fade. . . .

PULP 37

I wake up and do the chores that Doobe needs done while he works. Then I meet him down at

Leicester Square. We have a short one at the pub and then we jump on the train to Heathrow.

"I hope you didn't bring the hashish, Jimi."

"Of course I brought it . . . I thought we'd need it."

"What we DON'T need is a few years in a french prison because of a little miscommunication . . . Gimme it."

Doobe breaks the chunk in half and throws a half back at me.

"Cheers," he says and we toss the chunks in our mouths.

"Anything else I should know about?"

"Well . . . Yeah . . . I got the pipe."

"Gimme it."

I hand it to him, he breaks it up and throws it under the seat of the train.

The train lets us out right at Heathrow. We jump on to the plane and grab a glass of red wine, which is nice, because my throat is coated with hashish crumbs and I'm having trouble properly enunciating my vowels.

A trip to Paris—definitely some kind of justice I could have only earned in another lifetime.

"Doobe, this trip is fate . . . Man."

"No . . . It's about an hour and fifteen minutes," he says and turns out his overhead light.

I look out the window . . . Thinking . . . I got no right to even think about this life anymore . . . I don't know what the fuck is gonna happen . . . Nothing ever goes the way I THINK it'll go . . . Why do I even bother . . . The English Channel below me . . . Lined with lights . . . France on the other side . . . FUCK IT . . . FUCK GUILT . . . I'm gonna let it be whatever . . . NO MORE GUILT . . . NO MORE BULLSHIT . . . I'M GONNA DO WHAT I CAN DO WITH WHATEVER I GOT . . . OR WHATEVER I CAN GET . . . MY SLICE OF THE PIE . . . THE CITY OF MOTHERFUCKIN' LIGHTS AND LOVE . . . PARIS!

We land.

"Doobe, are you feeling that hashish?"

"Yahuh."

We hurry through the airport and find our way lost outside. WAY LOST! Neither of us speaks a word of french. I mean I studied it for years, but I don't even let Doobe in on that little piece of information, because between the hashish and my study habits in school, I'm useless. Doobe moves fast, being a New York boy, even though he's lost. I follow with my head on a swivel, lookin' like one of those big spring-head dolls that sits on top of a dashboard. London's Jersey City compared to PARIS! Sculpture . . . The whole fuckin' town. I think they commission artists to do the goddamn drinking fountains! Doobe hasn't said anything yet, but from what I can tell, we're walking in some kind of a tweaked circle. Finally, he turns.

"I don't know where we are."

"Did you just realize that? . . . We've passed this same fruit stand three times."

"Why didn't you fuckin' say something?!"

"Doobe, I have NO idea where we are. I don't even know where we SHOULD be going."

"Jimi . . . I'm really spun from that hashish. I didn't realize it until now."

We walk a while, until we hear a few words of english, and ask directions. Lucky for us, all the circling we did kept us close to where we needed to be. We're back on track. I begin to hear all the foreign tongues more as music than as a wall. It's actually better to not know what people are saying. I like it. London is one thing but Paris . . . Forget about it . . . The trip just started. London was a warm-up. I wanna go to Africa and India, that's the shit right there. Different clothes, and smells, and faces and teeth. It's all just started. It makes me think that maybe there are a few things worth living for! Maybe there IS something left after your first legal drink.

"We musta walked outta the wrong side of the airport."

"I'm glad you figured it out . . . I wouldn'ta even been able to dial a phone to call Jane."

"You woulda figured it out if you had to."

"Doobe . . . You're better at this stuff, trust me."

A little compliment and your average slob will bend over backwards for you. Just let Doobe believe that he IS the trailblazer and I'll never even have to open a map.

Ten minutes and one train later, we're in front of Jane's apartment. From what Doobe tells me, her dad is like some CEO-type who got hit by the mid-life crisis and decided it was time to spend some of his money on something other than Saabs for his five daughters, so he and the old lady packed up and moved to Paree. Jane, being the middle child and naturally, the most clueless, came over to "get her shit together." Yikes . . . To even put that cliché in quotes makes my herpes itch.

I met Jane for the first time at Ray's funeral, and I gotta come clean on this one . . . It was bad spooky voodoo vibes right from the get-go. The chick bummed me out hard. I mean I know that it wasn't her fault that slick-boy strung himself up in the old oak, but it being the only time I'd met her, it was hard not to associate Ray's death with meeting Jane. Something in my gut, knotted lie detector that it is, gave me a jolt when I touched her. I never believe what my gut tells me at first but that's probably a lot of the reason why I find myself SO WRONG all the time. As fucked up a human as I am, the animal part of me does OK.

Jane was all over the place at the funeral, blabbering and moaning and yelling, "Please don't take him! Don't close the door! Don't take him away," when they were shutting the casket, and that voice in my head was saying, "Shut the fuck up and have a yogurt or something, Jane!" I just don't know what it was. But you know Doobe thinks she's great, of course, like I said before, and that's why we're here. And forget about the rumors that Jane and Doobe have a thing going . . . Just forget about them.

We ring the bell. Mom answers and buzzes us in

and now here we are, all gook-eyed, meeting the family.

"Doobe! Oh my God! You made it!" she says, as if it's a miracle. "And Jimi! Oh my God! It's so good to see you again," as if we go way back. It's begun already.

Mom and Dad are alright. Dad's one of those banker guys who's decided it's time to get into the Arts, so he's moved to Paris, and Mom is definitely that faded Jane Fonda-esque debutante from like Long Island or maybe, the Oranges in New Jersey. A 1980s health spa version of Holly Golightly—the pearls, the hairdo, all slipped into a yummy-mummy motif. Nice enough people, and more importantly, they've cooked up a beautiful spread for us. Chicken, roasted with asparagus and potatoes and greens. Out of the corner of my roving eye, I see strawberries and cream waiting on deck in the kitchen.

Doobe's in rare form, the hashish that made me a zombie made him Jerry Lewis, so he carries the conversational ball, and tells of all our WACKY mishaps on the way to Paris. The parents love it, like they always do. I guess after a couple of decades on the couch ANYTHING can be pretty zany. I'm useless. I just have seconds and thirds, occasionally grunting or nodding my head to validate one of Doobe's twists. He lies a little, but the story moves better that way.

Jane, of course, is all but totally enthralled by every peep Helms makes.

"Did you really? . . . Oh my God! . . . And you weren't scared?!" The thing that bothers me the most about Jane is that it's obvious she WAS perfect for Ray, and I can't bear to see that simple truth bouncing around in front of me. Even with my iron curtain of humor, it's painful to watch her bounce around in front of me, thinking of old purple Ray. Ray'd found the perfect playmate. All the right stuff, that earthy rich girl from the east hanging out in Aspen, hiking and skiing, waiting tables, going to Dead shows and doing bucketsful of coke—just perfect for him.

Mom and Jane finally clear the table and I watch with a broken heart as the last few potatoes escape my jaw-full death.

"You two boys shower, and then we're going out." I wanna tell them to go on without me so I can stay home, eat the leftovers, and make passes at Mom, but something tells me to hold back.

PuIp38

We walk through the city, Doobe and Jane laughing while I swing in and out of insecurity. It's either, "what a coupla assholes," or "oh jeez, I wish they'd talk to me" the whole way.

"We'll go to Harry's. You guys'll love it. They serve whiskey there and the walls are filled with pennants from american colleges."

"That sounds cool," Doobe says.

"Yeah, that'll be cool," I say, thinking, Yeah . . .

Wow . . . Yippee . . . Great . . . Really . . . College banners and everything? The false promise of bonding with a bunch of american students over in Europe is almost too much.

We walk in and there it is. Just like Jane said. We could be in any bar on the yuppified Upper West Side of Manhattan, my only consolation being a Gold Card that Jane drops onto the bar.

"Tab please."

I now . . . Love Jane.

The free-flowing booze softens my black heart towards Jane. I begin to see her in a new light—a mash-enlightened light. She's a lush. No surprise, but always still nice to see. One shot after another, with the confidence that comes from a lifetime of spending daddy's money. We gain, much to my chagrin, two young french idiots into our clique, both of whom make it their business to make a run on Jane. I'm tired and I could care less as long as they don't bump my arm while I'm drinking. But after awhile, their putrid flirtations embitter me. Doobe's trying to "get to know them," thinking that maybe he just "doesn't understand them," but I'm in no mood for such cultural sluttery. I think they're ASSHOLES! Last Call comes and goes and I finally step in.

"Jane . . . Ah, maybe we should go now?"

"Yeah . . . Jane . . . Jimi's right . . . We are actually kinda tired from the trip . . . Maybe we could go home now?"

"Yeah . . . OK . . . ," she says. "Nice meeting you guys . . . We're gonna go now."

And that's when it happens. . . .

"OOhhh cum onnn . . . Yew are nut go-ink to let theesse friennnzzz . . . Tell yew zwhat tu duuu . . . Are yuuuu?!"

She snaps and I see.

". . . Ummm . . . Yeah . . . I mean no!!!" She barks, "I want to stay . . . Nobody tells me what to do!"

Need I write anymore? Right in front of me, in all her glory, is the ballbusting cunt who, in my mind, pushed Ray into the noose when she shoulda pulled him out of it! Like a lightning bolt of "I told you so's!" Right in front of me. We end up staying another hour, bribing the bartender for shots and listening to these two french assholes make bogus small talk. It's all I can do to drink the bitch's booze! Doobe's literally asleep. The only reason I stay awake is because I've become so hateful towards Jane.

In the end, Jane blows off both the swishy Paris boys, and we hail a cab home. Doobe and Jane go into her room "to talk," and I sneak into the kitchen to eat. The potatoes are gone! There isn't a goddamn thing in the house except for some ancient pine nuts, which I gobble down. After all the salt is licked off the bag, I tiptoe over to the couch, take off my clothes and go to bed. . . .

"Oh Fuck! . . . Jimi . . . You gotta put those boots outside . . . And wash your feet!"

"What?"

"I can smell those things in Jane's room . . . This whole place stinks!"

"Thanks . . . Buddy," I say, getting up. "I guess they are a little ripe, aren't they?"

"Peaches are ripe . . . Those things fuckin' stink!"

PULP 39

"Urgh . . . Uuuuchhhhhh . . . Joooook . . . Galoop . . . !" Jammed into a little white shitter, I scrape and pull at the bottom of my stomach. I got the bad pine nut flu! Every once in awhile I muster a little bile, but mostly it's just wretching painful dry heaves. I taste the nuts with every heave. Hanging on to the edge of the cold porcelain bowl, my face thrust over the murky water, I taste the nuts, again and again. If I could just drink some ginger ale . . . If I could just remember what life was like before I started puking . . . I can't . . . There was no life before this . . . I was born . . . They stamped a 9-digit number on my forehead . . . And I caught the bad pine nut flu . . . That's what it is . . . That's what happened . . . Now I remember . . . I've had this bad stomach from day 2 . . . The pain . . . Ohh-hhhhhhhh . . . Again . . . Uuuuurrrggghhh . . . Ssplunk . . . Ooooowwww . . . Jjjjjaaaaa . . . Sswash . . . Over and over . . . I want my mom . . . I wanna be a baby again . . . I want permission to cry . . . Zzzzzoooowwwwww . . . Oooooccc-cooooookkkk . . . And all that guttural hemming and hawing and what do I get . . . Two green chunks the size of rabbit turds . . . The only nice thing is that Jane's parents are outta the house . . . I wanna scream . . . I wanna puke my way back to the womb . . . There's no dignity . . . There's no dignity when the chunks hit the bowl . . . Hit the bowl and splash back up in my face . . . Murky puke-water slime dripping off my chin . . . Spitting . . . Trying not to swallow down any of the slime . . . This's HELL . . . This is truly HELL . . . Those fuckin' pine nuts . . . Out the window it's balmy . . . All the world's happy but me . . . Everybody's taken the day off and is playing in the park but ME . . . No relief . . . I puke until I can't breathe . . . I sit back . . . Start to sweat . . . And then . . . I gotta do it all over again . . . I puke an hour for a moment's joy . . . No relief . . . I'll just ride it out . . . Think about funny things . . . The Marx Brothers . . . They're supposed to be funny . . . Ooooooooooooooooooooooooooohhhh fuck . . . UUURRRGGGHHH . . . Aaaaaalllllluuu-uuupppppp . . . UUURRRGGGHHH . . . ZZZZZ OOOCCCCKKKKK . . . Always back to UUUR-RRGGGHHHH . . . All the world is happy . . . Everything is sunny . . . And my mom has forgotten me . . . Strawberries . . . Here it is . . . There's no peace . . . I wanna eat a peach . . . Juicy . . . I can't remember how long it's been since I ate . . . Since I could eat . . . It's chicken broth for the rest of my life.

"Jimi . . . Are you OK in there?"

"Yeahqq . . . Pretty muchqqqqq . . . "

No end . . . A day . . . A life . . . I'm in HELL! "Doober and I are gonna go out and get some juice . . . Do you want anything?"

"Ginger ale . . . Pleaseqqqq . . . ?"

I hear the door close . . . I begin to cut loose . . . Scrapping and pulling . . . Wanting it to end . . . Looking for one of those motherfucking gods again . . . LOOKING AGAIN. . . .

PULP 40

Jane's on the telephone in the kitchen. Doobe's in the bathroom. I sneak into the master bedroom. It's a small room, clean to the point that it's got a Pine-Sol mist wafting about in the air. A small double bed with a powder-blue quilt takes up the back corner of the room. I have to stop and imagine Mom and Dad getting it on before I make another move. Jane's mother's quite the 40-ish looker—that air of wisdom sautéd lightly in a been-around-the-block tapenade. I can see her now, soothing poor Papa Bankerman's woes with her tanned fingers and those knowing taut thighs.

Back to business. I'm not here to wank it in some

soiled Bloomies cotton panties. THIS IS A MISSION. I spot the dresser and I make my move, listening carefully to the outside; keeping audio track of what's going on with Jane and Doobe. Of course, there's the required family pix on the top of the dresser. Jane's got some nice sisters. Jane's the petite one. All the other sisters are broad, jock-types. That's OK, where I grew up, a girl could throw a softball or two. I'm used to that active model—the tomboy. I want a woman who can rope a cow if she has to. Anyways, the dresser's got five drawers. I go for the top one . . . T-shirts . . . No dice . . . The second down . . . Boxers . . . What's the point? My jeans are already so cruddy . . . The third one . . . BINGO . . . SOCKS GALORE . . . Colored socks . . . White socks . . . Wool socks . . . Silk socks . . . Argyles . . . Plaids . . . This guy doesn't fuck around! I've got a new respect for Jane's father! I mean I'd seen him in some nice royal-blue tweedy socks, but who knew? The guy's got depth! I select a pair to my liking . . . Nothing special . . . A knee-high tube . . . Goes a long way. I slip them on . . . My feet are squeaky from the shower . . . Yes . . . Better than a sauna and a rub down . . . My feet love me . . . It's been a while . . . Things were bleak in London . . . Doobe doesn't do enough laundry . . . I debate whether or not to grab a thick purple wool pair for the road, but decide against it on the grounds that I think it would show no class . . . Take what you need, Jimi . . . Not what you want . . . And sneak back out into the living room, flopping down with a magazine I can't read.

Jane comes out of the kitchen.

"You look a lot better today, Jimi."

"Feel a lot better too, Jane."

"Doobe's gone out to get some wine. I told him to get you some more ginger ale."

"Jane, you're a good woman."

"I'll be in the shower if anyone calls for me."

"Ok . . . Jane . . . Is it alright if I try to get in touch with that guy, Harry, I told you about?"

"Sure . . . Mom put instructions for dialing out next to the phone," she says, and closes the bedroom door behind her.

"Thanks a lot," I yell back, and go into the kitchen. I call the school that Harry goes to, and they say that they can't give me his number but that they'll take a message and give it to him. I promise that I'm not a rapist but to no avail. I leave Jane's number and hang up. Doobe returns with ginger ale and vino.

"You look a lot better today, Jimi."

"Better than I looked when I was lapping up water out of the commode?"

"Exactly . . . Have some ginger ale. I got some broth I'll heat up for you."

I sit back on the couch while Doobe heats up the soup. Life is good again, sipping on soda with clean thick socks on, not puking my guts up.

Pulp 41

Notre-Dame standing tall in the middle of Paris—a monument to years of Christian suffering and terrorism reduced to a stop on a guided tour. There's a big crater in front of it where some Nazi bomb landed. The locals say it's a miracle, the bomb that is. Burn the fucking building, and save a few million people, I say. Faith.

"Let's go in and light a candle for Ray," Doobe says earnestly.

"Definitely . . . Don't you think so, Jimi?" Jane chirps.

"I'm not adverse to a little prayer." Might be a good time to look for some help with my stomach virus.

We walk inside the massive wooden front doors and sit down at a bench along the wall.

"I'll get us a candle to light."

Jane and I sit in silence while Doobe trots over to a divinely inspired huckster and gets a candle. He comes back and sits down next to Jane. Not a word is spoken for what seems like hours until finally, Helms turns with tear-streaked eyes.

"Come on . . . Let's go over to that side altar," and takes hold of Jane's hand.

My first impulse is to say, "Hey, if we're gonna light one last one for our man, shouldn't we at least go to the center altar and get a straight-on audience with the Man?" but I don't say it. The truth is that I got the emotions flowing. I let the corniness slide. For a moment I stop being "the guy with the funny line" and I let this thing be whatever it is. I see Jane for the first time . . . For the pained soul that she is. The look in her eyes and the sadness in her face . . . Whether or not she could have helped is neither here nor there at this point. She cared about Ray. The only thing getting in the way is that she's as fucked up as he was! We're all as fucked up as he was! It's no secret . . . THIS LIFE . . . Probably takes out most of us.

Doobe motions to Jane to come up and join him at the altar. I stay behind, not knowing if they want me to be RIGHT there with them. I'm here, more or less, as a witness, but that's alright. I'm here. Doobe lights a long wooden match, bringing it up in front of him and Jane, illuminating their faces . . . The match ignites with a leap . . . The flame stretching bright . . . And then settles into a steady burn . . . Looking soft . . . Looking kind . . . Free . . . For just a second . . . Of all my fear . . . And my suffocating judgments . . . I see Doobe . . . I see Jane . . . I see Ray . . . And I see me . . . Climbing upwards . . . The flame . . . But always dying back down again . . . Jane puts her little-girl hand . . . In need of a cigarette . . . On Doobe's hand . . . And they reach out to the candle in front of them . . . I watch as the wick scorches . . . And then accepts the fire. . . .

RITUAL

SILENCE

What is a hero but a silly prelude to a tragedy . . . A victim . . . Built up and torn down like so many billboards on Hollywood Boulevard. A need for more and bigger, leaves no choice. Ray's gone and we're lighting a candle, trying to make ourselves feel better, or bring back some part of him. Sitting there watching a flame burn, wishing I wasn't puking so much . . . Wishing I was drinking in a dark bar . . . Drinking with Ray . . . Drinking with anyone . . . But I stay . . . And sit . . . Doobe is crying . . . And Jane is crying . . . And I'm wishing . . . Wishing that I could cry . . . The tears locked behind some thing . . . Some wall . . . I can't see . . . Wishing a candle could change anything . . . Errol Flynn was a faggot, I see . . . Marilyn Monroe was a junky, I hear . . . And JFK was a slut, I speak . . . My old man once asked me what I believe in and I shrugged . . . Thinking I'd be an asshole to say anything other than "I don't know." A test. I really don't know . . . I just remember . . . Ray . . . Laughing . . . Talking . . . Walking . . . Being alive . . . Being my friend . . . He was such a doomed fool to begin with . . . The guy never did anything right . . . The last time I saw him alive he was standing in front of a group of people outside the fraternity . . . Impressing them . . . I remember thinking . . . Poor Ray . . . When's he ever gonna get over it . . . I barely spoke with the guy . . . I just wanted out of school and as far away from all those people as I could get . . . HIS CHOICE . . . He made a choice . . . A BIG LAST STAND . . . And now here I am in Europe on some false little pilgrimage, trying to recapture some lost light. . . .

The credits are rolling on the Ray movie and we're walking out the door in a Day-Glo shroud of tears. The sun is going down on the ancient streets of Paris, and all the women look so kind in the streets. I want to grab them and kiss them. I grab Jane and kiss her.

"Jane, he'd be psyched about this."

"He is."

I start to blush. The blood inside me pumping through my face. Not caring. Seeing this world, and seeing Ray. Loving the women, and hearing the music. Not being afraid to hold a small piece of it for once. Not being afraid of losing or failing. I'm in love with the pain, and the joy, and all the in-between stuff. So much of it is in-between. Realizing my smallness and being glad I don't really have anything to do with the outcome of a whole day on this planet. Watching the world and drinking from its filthy gold cup . . . Not because I can . . . But because I do. . . .

Pulp 42

A figure appears across the park. I watch as the body comes into focus, zigzagging between winos and fountains—Harry Clements. Harry walks with his feet low on the ground, shuffling side to side like all hockey players walk. Feet down along the ground, pushing off to the side with hips rolling, waiting for a puck, or a pass, or a hit. I get up from my spot next to Doobe and make my way over to meet him.

"I didn't know if you'd get that message or not."

"Yeah, I got it right away, but I had some things I had to get done and I didn't wanna call you until I had them outta the way."

I pull him in with a hug.

"I kinda needed to split for a couple of days. I'm caught in this family thing and it's driving me crazy."

"I thought this guy, Helms, was your buddy?"

"He is . . . It's just, I've been with him at this girl's place with her mom and dad . . . And I'm getting fucking antsy . . . Come on over and meet them."

We walk back over to Doobe and Jane, and I

introduce Harry. I don't know Harry all that well myself, but he goes out with an old friend. When I met him, we connected right away. I need Harry. I gotta get away from Doobe and Jane for awhile. I'm sick of the *All in the Family* scene with the family. I'm broke again. All the uncle's money's gone, and I need some new wells to tap into. I figure Harry's lonely for some back-home companionship, and we can hang out for a couple days. Everybody will be happy. Doobe and Jane can do their thing and I'll go do mine.

We sit down and pass the wine. Jane keeps on saying, "Ray would've loved this." It's her latest profound discovery. After Notre-Dame, Ray's come "to love" everything that happens to the three of us. I'm beginning to get worried about her. There's a twisted look in her eyes every time she mouths the phrase. Doobe and I've gotten to the point where we just look at each other and shrug when she says it. The girl needs help and I can't pay lip service to the communal mourn. I'm out the door. Let Doobe handle it.

"So yeah . . . Harry knows all the same people we know," I say, evoking a bond. "Went to U. of Maine with all your buddies from home, Doobe."

"Do you know———?"

"Yeah and———."

A network of fuck-ups looping the globe. People roaming lost and looking. Hiding out in all the most picturesque places the world has to offer, killing time. Everybody knows someone, and if they don't, then they know someone else who does—it's the "do you know" game. Perfect for immediate comradery. Names are tossed back and forth and the wine is passed. I sit back and listen, closing my eyes. All I can see is that little spot of red you see when you close your eyes facing the sun. Letting my friends and their friends meet, while I relax and drink. It's nice to be in Paris. In five years, I hope I just remember the good parts. The sun and the park and the conversation and the children playing and the winos being warm on the grass. Me, just sitting back with my eyes closed and my head cupped in my hands, looking at the red screens. I don't wanna talk.

The sun goes behind the clouds and the bottles run dry. Harry wants to get going, we gotta meet some friends of his at a bar across town, so we get up to leave. I look down at Doobe and Jane and my melodramatic engines kick in. I wanna get away from them and yet, I feel like I'm abandoning them.

"I'm going back to London in two days, I gotta work this weekend."

"Harry'll be sick of me by then, anyways . . . I'll call you."

"Jimi, I'm glad you came and stayed with us. My parents thought you were funny."

"I had a good time. We'll call you tomorrow and see what you're up to," I tell them.

Doobe says, "No problem." But he knows this is it. I think he gets the vibe. We say our good-byes and I start walking away with Harry.

"Don't forget to call us!" Jane yells and I wave back. I always say I'll call. It's a lot easier than having to say good-bye.

PULP 43

Harry and I walk for about two miles through the city. We gotta stop and pick up a friend of his, and then we're meeting some other people at a place called the Crown.

"He's a good guy," Harry assures me. My head immediately translates that into "a guy who will have some food and beer for me and maybe a chunk of hashish."

It ends up that the guy lives in the 7th district, not too far away from Jane's parents. He's not home and we wait on his stairs.

"Harry, do you ever miss the states?"

"I did for awhile . . . Until one day I realized that I didn't really have anything to go back to . . . I mean, I flunked out of every college I went to and I've been away from home for so long that that's the last place I want to be now. . . ."

"I feel like I have everything to go back to . . . I just don't wanna go back to it."

"Paris is kind of surreal . . . It's like I don't age here or something, because everything's so different to begin with . . . Back home, I'd always be thinking about what I should be doing and shit . . . It doesn't fucking matter here."

Harry sees a guy coming towards us and gets up.

"I thought you were gonna be here . . . We've been here an hour!"

"I did not say that I would be home before six o'clock, Harry."

"Flavio, this is Jimi."

"Hi, Flavio."

"Nice to meet you, Jimi."

Flavio looks spanish. He's light-skinned, tall and skinny, dressed in natty clothes—kind of a fashionable guy, and his hair is slicked back tight on his skull, perfectly. We follow him up two flights of stairs to his apartment, a big loft with framed prints on every wall and a thin black leather couch in front of a lone onyx table.

"Nice fucking place you got here, Flav."

"Thank you, it is my father's but he is only here one week a year. He's an art dealer. He travels very much."

"That explains the prints, I guess."

"My father is very fond of your american artists."

"Lichtenstein?"

"Yes. He is his very favorite painter."

"I always liked the whole cartoon thing myself."

"Very powerful."

"And funny too . . . That's big."

Harry returns from the fridge with some beers.

"Jimi, this is som'a the finer french lager," and

hands me an open beer. Flavio returns from the kitchen with a long-stemmed, glass, hashish pipe.

"Welcome to Paris . . . Please do us the honor."

I take a swig offa my beer and hold the pipe up to my mouth as Flavio so graciously gives me a light. I take a hit. The hashish is powerful. I'm thrust back instantly to my first bong hits in junior high. Sitting behind the local church, thinking my old man was gonna walk around the corner at any minute and ground me for the decade.

"Strong . . . Isn't it."

"Strong . . . I'm ready to call up my parents and apologize for everything I've ever done . . . This shit makes me feel like a child molester or something."

"It does have sort of a PERVERSE air doesn't it, Jimi?" Harry adds. "Our friends travel quite a bit . . . Some of the guys we're meeting later on just got back from Turkey with this stuff."

"No wonder those people never make it out of their robes."

We drink our beers and pass the pipe, listening to some sitar music that Flavio just picked up. I'm not crazy about the music but I keep my mouth shut about it. I don't want to insult Flavio's well-intentioned hospitality. At least not until I've stuck my head in the fridge. Harry's flipping through a print book and Flavio gets on the phone to sure up plans for the evening. I start to play with a little grey kitten that's been darting around the room. Flavio looks up from the phone.

"Her name is Zooey . . . Like the Salinger story." Flavio loves to drop a name here and there.

"Come here Zooey . . . Come here girl," I say, beginning to crawl on the floor. "Come here baby . . . Come on."

Zooey is shy and she continues to dodge me. Flavio is on the phone and Harry is lost in his book and I start to chase this little cat. "Come on Zooey . . . Come on over here."

The cat doesn't want anything to do with me, but finally I get her in a corner and come up close to her. I lean my face down in front of her and make kissing noises.

"Come on little one . . . Smooch smooch . . . Come on." WHAM! She catches me with a paw right across my cheek. Rage fills my face with blood. I grab her in my hands and flip her over onto the ground. I'm furious! The little slut scratched me! I look back over my shoulder. No one's looking and I begin to squeeze her, the soft fur in between my fingers. She looks up at me, frightened, and I grab her around the throat, twisting her head to the side, pulling at her throat. I wanna kill the little fuck! I take another glance over my shoulder and still no one has looked over at me. I continue squeezing and the kitten starts to struggle with more intensity. Her eyes look away from me. I figure she's starting to realize that maybe her life is in danger. A wave of nerve runs the length of her torso with a jolt . . . She's now fighting for her life. I lean close to her. "I'm your god right now . . . Your life is in my fucking hands," and continue to twist and squeeze while she desperately shows her claws and tries to scratch her way out of the mess she's got herself into. She's put herself in a real bad situation. Little kitty yelps sneak out from between my fingers.

"Jimi . . . Do you want another beer?"

"What? . . . Oh yeah . . . Yeah . . . Yeah, I'd love another one."

I let go of the little cunt and she tears across the room into the closet. I turn around and Harry's coming towards me with a beer.

"You OK? . . . Jimi . . . You look a little flushed."

"Yeah . . . Oh yeah . . . I'm fine," I stammer and take the cold beer from his outstretched hand. I take a sip and try to regain a little composure while Harry goes over to fill another pipe. The beer's dark and thick—high-octane mud. I take a few more sips and I realize I'm shaking. Some kind of rush, maybe an adrenaline-shame speedball or something. Zooey's hiding under the couch and Flavio sits back down on the couch.

PULP 44

Everything in life seems worth the trouble as I walk through the swinging doors of the Crown. The place is so classic that my vision goes black and white the minute I set eyes on the bar. Time stops and I hear those beautiful horns again, just whispering and crying back in time. The bartender, bored, leans over on his handlebar moustache and checks his watch, ignoring us. There's even a sad blonde at the end of the small bar with a glass of half-drunk red wine and an ashtray full of cigarettes. The barkeep straightens his black vest and asks Flavio a question in french. Flavio answers, the guy runs both hands through the week-old-looking grease in his hair, wipes his hands on a rag that he pulls from his waist, and reaches down to put three glasses down in front of him on the bar. We sit down behind the glasses and I get my first of many Calvos. It's an apple liqueur, and we chase down the shots with espresso. The juke box only plays french tunes.

"What are they saying in this song?" I ask.

"They're all singing about Love and Loss."

Down with the Calvos, and back up with the espresso, all night long, listening to songs I can't understand the words to, only feeling them. It's nighttime and I stir brown cubes of sugar into my espresso, sitting in the Crown. I can only hope the sun never comes up again. A bunch of other spanish guys show up, and Flavio joins them. Harry introduces me to them but we stay off to the side on our own.

"You know, Harry . . . I never thought life was gonna be like this . . . I mean I kinda wanted it to be like this . . . In Europe and everything . . . But you know it's different from what I THOUGHT it would be like."

"I never thought I'd live here . . . But I love it now."

"Sitting in this fucking place makes me forget everything."

"Now you get it. . . ."

"I could die here."

"I'm sure you wouldn't be the first."

"You know, Harry . . . I'm a little short on cash."

"Don't worry about it . . . My treat tonight . . . I'm glad you called me."

"I'm glad I called you, too."

"It's nice to get someone over here to hang with now and then . . . We'll have a good time . . . Just drink and enjoy yourself."

I'm filled with forgetting . . . Sweet . . . And simple. No more cats will cry in my hands tonight.

PULP 45

Wrapped in a thin veil of dusty cloth, with a throat of sand and a deaf nose, I roll over. I gotta go, my bladder is a pregnant balloon. Where the fuck am I? Paris . . . The rest is questionable. I check to make sure I don't have some once-beautiful pig next to me that I gotta crawl over without waking up. I don't wanna have to perform. I'm as far from sex as a chronic masturbator can be. I have to dump bad.

I get up and walk out a door. I see Harry sleeping in an alcove and I feel remotely safe. There's a small shitter in the foyer between us. I'm definitely in the SMALLEST apartment I've ever seen—two closets fused together, walkway and a toilet. We're high up, many stories. There's a window in the bathroom that looks out over a whole side of the city. At least fifteen stories, no broken neck on the landing of that jump. I imagine it'd be clean. What a view.

I sit down and the valve that is my sphincter opens. Buckets of glass squirting sour. I'm pissing out my ass. It's painful but not as bad as the pain of holding back. Every once in awhile, some kind of metal peanut flies out and tears at the wall of my butt. All the buildings are wet, the city looks rested. I can't see any people from where I sit, just windows, stone, and some brick. I let out some gas. A long balloon-on-the-loose kind of fart, and another pocket in my bowels cuts loose. PURE JOY. It smells bad. Am I getting rid of the bad stuff? Or is this an indication that there's MUCH bad stuff inside? My head goes back to the Crown, something about a faded lily of a bleach-blonde, telling me the story of her life, while I try to gauge whether or not she likes me. Does she tell everyone the story of her being raped by her brother, or does she trust me? Flavio appears in my mind, briefly, handing me another Calvos, toasting Lichtenstein's cartoons. It's the first real triumph of my alleged college education—a free shot of booze for some rudimentary art history facts. It was all worth it, Dad. A few more farts and then what feels like swollen sand pellets begin to squeeze out of my butt in sequence—grainy strands of pearls. After a couple of minutes, the strings get shorter and the pebbles get smaller, until they pop out one at a time, and it ends. I look around to see, much to my chagrin, that there isn't any *papier du toilette.* The injustice calls tears to my ducts. It isn't fair! This shit is not fair! I can take a lot of things, but this is just too much! What the hell did I do that's so wrong! Am I just a bad person or what?! There's nothing in the room! Not even a piece of cardboard! I look up next to the tiny sink, off to the left, and see a soiled glimmer of salvation—A single threadbare sock in desperate need of a good darn and wash. Such a precious commodity in the life of a young man like Harry or I, there's almost a factor of guilt, but I erase it immediately out of what I deem an ABSOLUTE NECESSITY. I gotta do it! It has to go! I take a long stern swipe and pull the rag up to my face. Brown, not bloody—A good sign. A few small seed-like remnants from an old meal. The smell is much more intense face to face. When I smell shit in the air, it smells bad because I'm expecting to smell air. When I smell it on a piece of toilet paper, it's more like a medical checkup or something, and it's not as bad, it's intense. The sock is a little stiff, so as I wipe, there's a certain amount of scraping involved to what is already a ravaged bung-scape. Yeah . . . It hurts! My face muscles turn stoic on me as I power through the last wipes, and then I follow it with a couple handfuls of water. Someday . . . I'll be able to fart again without whimpering. The sock . . . Now that's another story altogether. That baby's got no place to go but out the window. I open the latch and let it go . . . Watching as it flutters and rolls down past the other windows and buildings, until at last the angle is too severe and I can't see it anymore. I pull up my pants, wash my hands, splash cold water on my face, and take a gulp. I've done as much as I can to get rid of yesterday.

Pulp46

"This shit isn't all that smooth but it will wake a guy up."

"It's just what we need, Jimi . . . I don't think that standard american stuff will get us through this one."

Sitting in a cafe around the corner from Harry's place, next to about a dozen old men with no place to go. None of us are vagrants, we just don't have any place to go. Gagging down some espresso. Last night's Calvos shook me harder than I thought, and Harry's in worse shape than I am. It hurts to think. I felt better earlier this morning. This hangover just keeps growing. Noon might be unbearable! One of those sugar hangovers like from drinking those rummy foo-foo drinks all night long. The umbrellas are fun to twirl and everything, but the next-day price is way too high. Anyways, my head hurts in a particularly excruciating way. It longs for the days of Kool-Aid and posies. I don't think there's a coffee in the world that can pull me and Harry out of this one. The sun is out . . . And out . . . And out . . . And out! I could fry potatoes at my temples. Harry looks as miserable as I am, but takes it a lot better. He doesn't get all dramatic. When I'm in pain, I'm like a jewish chick from Long Island. I think the wincing and rolling around in my seat is making him feel better. We only stay for a single refill, and then we go back to the apartment and watch dubbed american soaps. I fall in and out of sleep curled up around a pillow. . . .

"I don't think we can shake this one, Jimi. We gotta go hair of the dog."

"The thought of that first Calvos makes me gag . . . But I'll gag it down and puke it up to get to the second one."

We run back around the corner and sit down again. The first shot crawls down my throat. I chase it down with sugary espresso. The magic cure's just around the bend. A couple of hours of artificial joy and then we're on our own again. The same group of men, all four cigarettes older, sits in the cafe.

"You know, Harry . . . I try to act as cool as possible . . . But the truth is . . . I don't know what the fuck I'm gonna do with my life beyond the next round of Calvos."

"I don't either . . . Are we supposed to?"

"No . . . I mean . . . Maybe not . . . But I'm starting to get real scared . . . Everything's like a symbol of my lost-ness . . . I sit down at a table . . . See a knife and a spoon crossed and I begin to sweat . . . Doom everywhere."

"Jimi . . . I came to Paris 'cause I got sick of answering all the same questions when I talked to my parents . . . You don't have to tell me . . . No one asks over here . . . That's why I love it here now . . . People over here know that everybody's clueless . . . It's like THE SECRET THAT NEVER CROSSED THE ATLANTIC."

"I think . . . Therefore I'm not."

Afternoon sets in and so does the crowd. I find myself staring deliciously at a set of young college breasts wrapped snug in one of those India-print hippy T-shirts. I can see the contour of the breast perfectly. Smooth, every bump around the nipple shows through. Breasts are so wonderful.

"Why don't you put your eyes back in your head, Pervert!"

I look up at her face, she looks at me with an almost angelic glow. It isn't until I spot ruddy-cheeked bull-dyke next to her that I trace the voice.

"My apologies . . . I didn't mean anything rude by it . . . They showed up in my line of vision and I lost myself."

"Yeah . . . Well . . . Maybe this'll help you find yourself." SWISH. I catch a face full of beer from the retarded girl-son of Martina Navratilova. I'm blinded for a second by the sting of the alcohol, then I freeze, wondering if I should be a total nonsexist, and break something over this bitch's head. When I open my eyes, all I find is Harry's laughing face. No breasts. No nothing. I shoulda smacked the brute when I had the chance to.

Harry goes up to the counter and comes back with a dishrag.

"Get cleaned up . . . You're in no shape to fight."

"Did you see what that dyke did to me?"

"Yeah . . . And I think you got away relatively unscathed . . . She had arms the size of your legs."

"I coulda taken her."

"Maybe . . . But you wouldn't have gotten the girl anyways."

PVLP 47

A friend of Harry's father has a daughter staying on the Île Saint-Louis. We jump on a bus into the middle of the city, and then walk across a bridge to the isle.

"Yeah . . . Her dad is the Donut King of Chicago . . . My dad tells me that she's worth a lot of money . . . She could be my ticket, Jimi . . . A lifetime of highly stylized worker's compensation!"

The Île Saint-Louis is beyond my wildest quaint old-world fantasies. I don't know any french history, but I'm sure like half of it happened on the very cobblestone streets we walk. We find the address and ring the bell.

"Hello?" We look up and see two heads pop out the window above us. My first thought is, "Fat . . . I knew it!" Both girls leaning out the window have heads that are so fat, I only can imagine what their asses look like.

"How ya doin'? . . . My name's Harry Clements . . . Our dads are friends."

"Oh yeah . . . My dad said he'd given somebody my number, hold on a second, I'll come down!" says the homelier of the two.

"I guess it's too late to run now, Harry."

"I wish we knew that was their window . . . We coulda thrown rocks at it and got a look at'm before we rang the bell."

The doors open and all of a sudden, Harry and I are at the state fair. TWO HEIFERS.

"Hi, Harry . . . My name's Jenny . . . And this is my friend from school, Lisa."

"This's a friend of mine, Jimi."

We all shake hands and go up to the apartment—an amazing exposed-brick loft with a big fireplace. We sit down and the girls get us beers.

It turns out the girls are pretty nice. TYPICAL. It's that classic "fat girl with TONS of personality" scenario times two. The girls make us some pasta and we drink all night long. They've got a stocked fridge of good beer and wine. They're happy to have the company and Harry breaks out the hashish pipe. We smoke a few bowls and watch the street, under the loft. I make runs to the fridge while Harry keeps the pipe full. The night goes on and we all get pretty trashed and, of course, being in the company of students on drugs, a bogus artsy conversation erupts. Jenny, I guess the more literate of the two, starts in on this whole thing about how there aren't any great living poets. Over and over again, she shrieks, "There haven't been any great poets since the 60s!" "FUCK THE SIXTIES," Harry screams. ". . . A bunch of upper-middle-class white kids blowing their parents' money and not showering . . . Having lots of sex and thinking they're changing the world . . . THE WORLD HAS ALWAYS CHANGED BY FUCKING! . . . IT'S NO BIG DEAL . . . IF THE 60S CHANGED THINGS SO MUCH . . . HOW COME THE WORLD IS MORE FUCKED THAN EVER? . . . And anyways . . . Peter, Paul and Mary are playing the Vegas strip now if you wanna go hear 60s poetry." Good going, Harry. "Well . . . They tried at least," she pouts. "Yeah . . . You're right I guess," I say, not wanting to bite the hand that feeds me, too hard. Cheering inside and riding the fence on the outside. There's plenty more beer in that fridge and I'm pretty much void of political opinions anyways. Jenny continues on a whole tangent about how poetry is dead and everything else. Harry's off, deep into the fridge at this point, and starting to make some moves on Lisa. I watch outta the corner of my eye while he lays kisses on Lisa. The natural move for me is to make a move on big Jenny, out of respect for my boy. That way, Jenny won't be pulling Harry off Lisa when it gets late. I scoot over next to her big rump, stick an arm around her waist, pointing down at the street.

"That's poetry down there, baby," and give her a smooch on her cheek. She turns and looks at me with eyes of appreciation that only a fat, undersexed gal could have, and gives me a big wet one on the lips. My lips are waltzing with a couple sticky inner tubes, but I cling to that feeling, knowing and terrified that the tongue is next. I try to turn her around to face me but to no avail. I don't have the arms for it. Jenny realizes what I'm trying to do and rotates herself. It's ugly . . . But . . . I get into it. ALL FLESH. I've never played with flab like this in my life. Every part of her body is a maze of mush and folds. At one point, I'm actually pulling on a zit thinking I've found the nipple. We push back the coffee table and start to wrestle around by the window. Harry and Lisa are going at it hard over on the couch. The moans alone have my penis rigid and desperate. I start to maul Jenny . . . Or try to, at least, but she pulls a reversal and pancakes me with her gargantuan torso. I'm nothing compared to Jenny. She can swallow me whole and still want dessert. I got no say in the matter whatsoever. She grabs me by the hair and starts to lap at my face with a tongue, the likes I haven't seen since the old *Wild Kingdom* days. Marlin Perkins would kill for this footage! Jenny's no ordinary girl. She's got the tongue strength of a rabid St. Bernard. Her presence is so overpowering that I can't even work a substitution fantasy. I'M HERE WITH JENNY AND THAT'S THAT!

The rape of Jimi goes on for another forty-five minutes, until the tension has mounted and it's time to get down to it. I'm ready! Whatever this is, I'm in! She's a woman . . . I'm a man . . . Height . . . Weight . . . And shoe size don't matter . . . I'm breathing heavy . . . And ready to pull my rig out, when all of a sudden . . . The fleshy blanket is lifted and I see swollen fingers run through messy hair . . . The axe falls . . .

"We better not go any further than this tonight . . ."

"OK . . ." I say, thinking to myself, "Why is there gonna be ANOTHER NIGHT LIKE THIS!" But I refrain, looking for my jacket and boots. Harry's already by the door. I hop over next to him while trying to put my second boot on. Lisa comes back from the bathroom and gives Harry a long kiss. Jenny walks up to me and grabs my face, squeezing my cheeks together in a single hand and plants a final tongue-slap on me, and we more or less get pushed out the door.

Out in the street, I give Harry a shell-shocked look.

"Did you get laid?"

"No . . . Did you?"

"No . . . I got manhandled like no man has ever

handled me . . . I was into it and then . . . Boom . . . The rug got pulled!"

"We probably shoulda ran while we still had a chance," he says, and pulls two beers out of his coat.

Pulp 48

Champs Élysées, 2 A.M. Harry and I walk into a nice italian place and sit down.

"Do we have enough money to do this?"

"Jimi, I'm not sure we have enough money to do anything at this point."

"I'm fucking starved . . . Maybe we can just have a couple of appetizers . . . An antipasto or something?"

"Whatta ya got on you?"

"Harry . . . I don't have two pieces of change to rub and make noise with even."

"I got a couple bucks," counts, "enough for maybe a side plate of spaghetti and a small salad . . . That'll have to do."

A thin moustached waiter comes over, smiling.

"Can I get you gentlemen something to drink to start with?"

"Yeah . . . How about a couple Heinekens?"

"Merci," and leaves.

"Harry . . . What, did ya find another roll of francs in your sock?"

"No, Jimi . . . But I think we might have to wing this one . . . I'm fuckin' hungry."

"Chew and screw . . . I haven't done that since I was 12."

"I actually did it like last year . . . Sometimes that phone call home from France takes a coupla days to pay off . . . I was so hungry for like a week that I just started doing it."

"Well . . . I guess I'm up for it . . . I haven't had a good meal in a long time . . . That meal at the girls' place just stretched my stomach out and made me fuckin' hungrier . . . I almost passed on it for that reason, but it just smelled so good."

The waiter returns with the beers. "Are yu ready tu ordaire?"

"No actually, . . . Could you give us a minute?"

"Surely," and leaves again.

"Well . . . Whatta ya think, Jimi . . . Do we do it . . . Are you ready to do some running?"

"I'm hungry . . . I know that."

"Enough said," and gives the waiter the high sign.

The waiter returns, pen in hand, and Harry orders a full meal: minestrone soup, clams on the half, and ravioli. At that point, the food becomes free. We now, definitely, don't even have the money to cover Harry's meal. I order soup, marinated artichoke salad, fettuccine Alfredo with salmon and a bottle of modest red wine with the meal. I mean . . . If we're gonna do it . . . I might as well make it worth the consequences. The meal arrives and we eat like bulimic wolves. I'm swallowing the fettuccine in whole bunches, barely even chewing it after I spin it up in my big spoon. I steal a few clams from Harry and then offer him some artichokes. The wine tastes fine swishing around on my naive palate. I ordered the midrange stuff because I figure it's more believable coming from two young guys. The meal . . . Is excellent . . . A feast. We finally push our chairs back and make room for our expanding stomachs.

"Can I get yu tu anything else . . . Coffee . . . Dessert?"

"Ah . . . Yeah actually . . . Could we have some coffee?"

"No dessert?"

"Not right now, thanks . . . Maybe in a bit."

"Very well," he says, and disappears into the back of the restaurant.

"Well . . . Now's our chance Harr . . . I say we drink a cup of coffee, ask for a refill and to maybe see the dessert menu . . . As soon as he goes back for more menus we make our break."

"Sounds like a plan, Jimbo . . . You call the shots and I'll be right behind you."

"Yeah . . . Well, get in front of me once we get outside, because I won't know where to run."

We leisurely sip on our coffee while the waiter sits in the back of the restaurant at a table with the cook.

"I hope the cook doesn't get all excited and join in on the chase."

"Jimi . . . It'll all happen quick . . . The Champs Élysées is packed right now . . . All we gotta do is get in the crowd and we're home free."

We finish our coffee and I signal to the waiter to come up again with more coffee. He gets a fresh pot and refills us.

"We thought that maybe we'd like to see about a little dessert . . . Do you still have anything left this late?"

"Oh oui . . . We still have everything left . . . Let me get yu our dessert menu," the waiter says happily, thinking he's got some hearty eaters at his table.

"That would be great, thanks," I say.

The waiter starts walking back towards the kitchen through the aisle and Harry, the inside man, pushes out his chair . . . Just as it looks like he'll disappear into the kitchen, he stops and talks to his other table. Harry jerks back and the waiter turns his head our way. There's a frozen moment . . . Where it's like . . . We don't know if he's hip to what we're doing . . . Or if he's just looking back 'cause he heard a noise . . . My heart skips and butterflies rush into my stomach and start churning around the salmon and pasta I've just inhaled . . . The waiter then looks back at the table, continues talking, and then walks into the back. The cook is sitting at the last table near the kitchen but it's now or never.

"Hit it, Harry!" I say, and jump up from my

chair. Harry's already five steps ahead of me. I kick it out like I haven't done since my teenage vandal days. It's all I can do to keep up with Harry as he dives into the swirl of the Champs Élysées . . . I hear a few yells and turn my head . . . The waiter and the cook are at the front door of the restaurant but I look so quick that I can't even tell if they're chasing us or not . . . It hits me that I don't even have Harry's phone number . . . I never got it from him . . . So not only do I need to get out of the restaurant . . . But if I lose the guy . . . I don't know where I'm sleeping tonight . . . Or ever again, for that matter . . . I could be lost for days! I'm a radar . . . I follow Harry through the crowd with tunnel vision . . . Bumping into people . . . People I don't even see . . . I can't lose him . . . Christ . . . The guy won't let up . . . It goes on for what seems like a mile, until finally he ducks into an alley and I catch up.

"Are they after us?"

"I only turned around once, man . . . They were at the door . . . But I never heard or saw them after that."

"Jimi, I think that shit's all coming up . . . That meal was so heavy . . . That run just killed me!" he says, bent over with his hands on his knees, panting. I'm breathing hard and I can taste my meal again too. I haven't really had time to think about it until now, but Harry's right. It wouldn't be hard to puke at all. I put my hands down on my knees and start to take deep, long, controlled breaths, trying with all my might to hold down my meal. Harry starts puking. Ravioli, still intact, hits the pavement and slides across the alley. Big, long bursts shoot out from Harry's mouth. TECHNICOLOR YAWN. I struggle. Part of me wants to turn away, but the other part of me . . . Makes me watch. It's all I can do to enjoy the show and hold back my own feast.

Pulp 49

I wake up clinging to the dusty tapestry like we're old lovers. No sooner do I cover my face with a pillow to shield me from the treacherous daylight, when it hits me that I gotta catch a plane at 8 in the morning. Panic riddles my body as the reality strikes. I run into Harry's room to look for his watch. Harry's dead to the world. I grab his arm and twist it around so I can get a look at the time. It's 6:33. I drop Harry's arm back onto the bed. Harry hasn't so much as flinched up to this point. To tell you the truth, I'm glad. You see, somewhere in the middle of my parisian binge, Harry had expressed a desire to come back with me to London. At the time, I'd been like, "Oh yeah . . . That'd be awesome," because I figured it would keep the party rolling and Harry's wallet open. But now, facing the actual prospect of going back to London to a house that I'm not so sure still loves me quite as much as I'd like to believe, it's a different game. Especially since I sorta blew Doobe off when I hooked up with Harry and was sick of Jane. Yeah . . . All things considered . . . With just a few days left in London . . . I think it'd be better to go back without Harry and keep a low profile until my jumbo heads back stateside. The question is now . . . How do I get outta here without Harry feeling slighted.

I take a look at him. He looks beat. His skin's pale and he's got creases under his eyes. Maybe if I just get all ready to go, and then wake him up at the last minute, he'll be too rushed and he won't be able to rally? . . . If not . . . I guess I just have to tell him the truth . . . Oouch.

I run back to my room and throw my things into my knapsack: two shirts and my other jeans. I splash some cold water on my face and take a squirt of toothpaste to rub on my teeth with my index finger. The hair looks good with yesterday's grease still in it. I pull a quick comb through it and give a final adjustment with my hands. Fine.

"Harry . . . Harry . . ." I shake him. "Harry man . . . You gotta get up if you wanna go . . . You gotta get up RIGHT NOW!" I give him another good shake and his eyes squint. "Fuck . . . Jimi . . . What time is it?"

"I don't know, man, you got the watch . . . I think it's gettin' late." He looks.

"Man . . . It's almost a quarter to seven . . . What time does your plane leave?"

"Eight o'clock man . . . We gotta hurry."

Harry gets up in bed. I can see he's surveying the situation in his mind. I push again.

"Harry, we gotta go . . . Don't ya think . . . How far away is that airport . . . Can we make it, even?" I barrage him with panicky questions, everything I can think of that'll make him NOT want to come back with me. I watch his eyes, weighing, debating whether or not he should get out of bed.

"Jimi . . . I don't know man . . . I don't think I can make this flight . . . Maybe I oughta stay here and get my shit together for my classes?"

"You're gonna blow off London 'cause you got homework? Is that what you tellin' me?" I got him going right where I want him. It's a good time to turn it around and make it look like HE'S ABANDONING ME! "Well . . . Alright man . . . I can't MAKE you go I guess."

"I'm sorry, Jimi . . . I know I told you I'd go with you but I'm fuckin' exhausted and I gotta make sure I don't flunk outta school over here or my free ride's over."

"Fair enough, Buddy . . . Well this is it then . . . Thanks for everything," I say and with a quick hug I'm out the door 'cause I REALLY DON'T have much time to spare.

My last task is to score a pair of socks. There's a relatively clean pair lying next to Harry's dresser and I swoop them up on my way out the door. I throw them on in the foyer, taking off the pair I got at Jane's house. THEY STINK. I don't even wanna put them in my knapsack! What to do . . . What to do . . . Even in the garbage they'll ruin Harry's apartment. I turn around and spot a little fridge on a table next to the window. I open it. It's got a moldy half-lemon and a Styrofoam take-out container, open, with a rock-hard baguette and some cheese inside it. I throw the socks inside the fridge and shut it back up, he doesn't use the thing anyways, and head out the door.

Pulp 50

My only real problem at this point is that I have no idea how to get to the airport. Harry had said something about a bus that comes in front of his building every fifteen minutes, but I don't see a bus-stop sign anywhere. There's gotta be some kind of fucking *L'Autobus* sign or something, because in front of his building is one of those huge piazza-type things. I mean huge, like I don't think I can just stand in the middle and wait for the thing! I gotta pick my spot! I see a bum lying on a bench off to the side of the building and I figure the guy's bound to know. He probably fuckin' lives here. I walk over to him.

"Hey man . . . How ya doin' . . . Can you tell me where the bus stops that goes to the airport?"

The bum looks up at me and scratches his matted hair with a black-caked hand—the kind of filth that takes months, maybe years, to acquire.

"Je . . . Ah . . . Dui dui . . . Ah . . . Jenai . . . Adui . . ."

"Look man . . . I don't speak french . . . Ah . . . L'Autobus . . . Ah . . . Charles De Gaulle . . . I think . . . Je pense . . . Port de Aero . . . You know what I mean?" I gesture madly with my hands. He looks up at me and then looks back off to the side.

"Ah no we . . . Adey . . . New . . . La . . ."

"Look . . . Man . . . I told you I don't fuckin' speak the tongue . . . Port de Aero . . . Port de Aero . . ." I say and stick my arms out like they're wings. I start to circle the guy, saying, "Port de Aero . . . Port de Aero!" But to no avail. I get to thinking the guy's jerking me around. I look at him. He's smart. I'll bet he knows exactly what I'm asking, the motherfucker! I grab him. "Come on, you little lying bum motherfucker." I shake him back and forth, his eyes rolling in his head with every jolt, "Come on you fucker! What . . . Huh . . . You think you're not gonna tell me 'cause I'm american! I'll wring your fucking neck!" Right as I'm out of things to say . . . And basically, out of things to do . . . I mean, what am I gonna do, beat the guy up for not talking to me? I hear the sound of a large diesel engine across the way.

There it is! I drop the bum and grab my knapsack. I start running to the other side of the piazza, screaming, holding my arms up in the air. The bus driver sees me and holds. I run to the door, it opens and I bound up the stairs, give him my last francs that I got from Harry and sit down behind him. The bus driver counts the money and gives me a franc back, closes the door and pulls away from the curb. I look into the rearview mirror of the bus. Sweat's pouring down my forehead and everyone on the bus's looking at me like I'm some mad wino or something. I pull out a dirty T-shirt, mop up the face, and settle back into my seat.

PulP51

"So what you're saying is that you're an American who came here with no money, went to Paris with no money, and now you've come back to London with no money?"

"Exactly, Officer. . . ."

Back in the Customs Office, with my pants down at my ankles, giving the abbreviated version of my life story to a coupla cardigan sweater-heads. They're not buying it. As far as I know, I don't have any drugs on me, so I don't care. The only thing they can hold me for is being poor. I'm not sure, but I don't think they still have debtor's prison in London. They'll probably just make me go live in the streets and throw rotten vegetables at me. I got a tag team working on me—a real carbon copy of Laurel and Hardy. The fat one's in control, of course. He circles me, talking, while Skinny smooths my thighs and checks the soles of my boots. I'm a little shaken from my run-in with the wino in Paris. Between the wino and the cat at Flavio's, I almost feel like I still got a bicep. Anyways, now it's different, and I'm back at the mercy of these two bobby-school dropouts.

"Tell me . . . Mr . . . Banks . . . What would you have done without your 'friends' in Paris and London? How would you have gotten home?" says the fat guy.

"I don't know . . . I probably would've gone somewhere else where I had other 'friends.'"

"I see . . ." he says, unsatisfied with my calm and candor.

" 'E looks alright . . . 'E doesn't have anything on 'im," the skinny one says as he finishes checking my heels for secret compartments.

"Well . . . If I was one of your mates . . . I'd hate to put you up knowing you were bloody broke . . . Enjoy your stay in London . . . You're free to go," and the fat guy leaves, followed by his emaciated sidekick. I'm left alone in the stale neon office, feeling violated, to stuff my jeans back into my knapsack. I almost wanna piss on their grey carpet so the next guy can smell the customs boys for what they really are . . . SEWAGE. Chalk it all up as the downside of being a primarily law-abiding citizen.

The train back to Doobe's is almost empty. When

I get back to the flat, no one is home and I gotta sneak in through the side window. I make a pot of tea and with the luck of stoned Jesus, I find a stray piece of black hashish—oh, the beauty of shag carpeting. I pour myself a cup with honey and milk, cook up a bowl, turn on the tube, and fall into the glee of fuzzymentalstupidrevelry.

Pulp52

He gave me this armband. It's made of silver but it's real cheap. I love it though . . . It's part of my tribal vision of myself. I already had one armband, but then he, Rosie that is, gave me this one. At Doobe's restaurant there's a whole flock of queens who don't use boy-names. I think his "real" name is Richard but I only know him as Rosie. He's half and half, italian and scottish, and I'm half loaded.

"You're 24 . . . You're young . . . You've got all the time in the world to do whatever you want . . . Stay here and live with me mum and I . . . Please stay in London . . . Don't break ma heart!"

"You know, Rosie, . . . I just don't know about me, you, and your MUM . . . It might be a little too weird . . . All of us together . . . Probably be cramped too."

"We'll get our own place then . . . I'll do whatever, to make you happy!"

There it is, and I never even knew the bitch had a thing for me. How am I supposed to know? Who knew? In the midst of this Dickensian oblivion, a queen has fallen in love with me. Rosie wants me all to himself. It's an awkward situation, because every day, when Doobe goes in to work, I sit at that same pub next door, Gilbert and Sullivan, and mooch drinks off all the friends I've made who work with Doobe. Rosie's just gotten off his shift and he's got a purse full of pounds. All I can think of is how this guy could take me out on the town and we could rage until dawn. Dinner? . . . Drinks? . . . Dancing? . . . And then at dawn, he'd want to take me home and suck my dick. Or worse, he'd want ME to SUCK HIS DICK! What to do? Do I do it? Do I let this guy ride me like a pony for a few hours and let it all be just some groovy experience that I once had? Maybe I'll love it and become the biggest queen in England? Let this guy call me a bitch, grab me by my hair, and treat me like a tramp? Or maybe it'll be worse, and he'll sit there and caress me and tell me that he loves me and it'll have to be this beautiful thing? All just for a night out on the town?

Every time I get up from the table, he stares at me like I'm corn-fed veal. I have visions of myself being one of those wonderful high school sluts I grew up with, with the purple eye shit and the frosted hair. I'm the hunted. The ball is not in my court. I'm a slave to my excesses and yet, it's got nothing to do with me. It's Rosie.

A night of bourbon and all his tip money for the privilege of my company. Money for the powder room, for all you Holly Golightly fans out there.

"I'm serious, Jimi . . . I want you to stay with me!" he says with tones of urgency. The puppy-dog eyes, the soft stray touches, and then the best part, he sings me his favorite Janet Jackson song, putting me in the lyrics: ". . . Miss you, Jimi . . . I said I'll miss you much . . ." Over and over again, sadder and sadder with every sip of his drink. He's got that scottish brogue, so when he says "much," he says it like "muuuch," with an "ew" instead of an "ah." I can't take it, but I WILL take it as long as he doesn't start grabbing my crotch TOO INTENTIONALLY. I'll take every last drink and morsel of food that the queen'll splurge for! I'm not proud and if I am . . . Then I just won't tell!

I'd hung out with Rosie before many times, but we always just drank and Doobe was with us. We outnumbered him. But now things are even, and I'm in trouble. The thing that haunts me is that the guy told me once he wanted to come back in his next life as a sword swallower. Even my limited imagination-al facilities have huge vivid pictures of what this guy, Rosie, might be capable of. The thought of his dick nestled in the fold of my butt cheeks while he gives me a rubdown just gives me the . . . HEE-BEE-GEE-BEES! I just can't do it . . . But I can do it for awhile. I can do it as long as there's a table and at least one pair of blue jeans between us.

I finally agree, after many choruses of "Miss You Much," to go to his favorite italian eatery for a bottle of good red wine and a no-strings-attached meal.

To make him a fantasy in my mind . . . To make him like a beautiful young girl sitting in a cafe . . . Smoking like a man with man's clothes on . . . Sitting . . . Looking out . . . Looking with a face . . . A face so smooth . . . With skin so smooth like a face that's never wandered . . . I can look at that face . . . I can see that face and it makes me feel old . . . I feel old . . . Like I've lived on this planet for so much longer than Her . . . Or HIM . . . Or anyone other than those with the leather and glaze . . . I watch Rosie . . . Eating veal . . . While I eat liver and onions . . . It's succulent and I like watching Rosie eat his food, and he likes that I'm watching him, and we drink the wine, the good red wine . . . I'm floating again . . . I'm beyond this, I think . . . But I'm so very much in the middle of all this and that bothers me . . . It scares me more than anything . . . I'm so THERE and I don't know WHERE that is . . . How can I know anything when I don't even know WHERE or WHO I am? . . . I'm looking at Rosie and she looks beautiful, because I see her as he deserves to be seen . . . As a beautiful young girl, more innocent than me . . . Too innocent for me . . . I have my liver and onions and we drink wine . . . And we talk . . . And laugh . . . And then the meal's over, and we're at the train station and Rosie's looking at me, and the only thing left is a single verse . . . The part where I get my ass out of there, intact, with his tongue and his cock far away, sad, with Mum for another night, sadder. . . .

Rosie gives me a smile. He's a good person, maybe in another lifetime. I'm still in the habit of chasing down big, juicy pussies and things with a lot less hair on them, but I still love the guy. I just don't know him that well. He gives me one last hug.

". . . Oh Jimi . . ." I gather it's a "What could have been" kinda sigh, and he walks away.

Life gets real different. Two months ago, I'd fancied myself some young jockish rogue, slinging scotch, and drowning in little rich girls. Now, it's midnight, and I'm watching a melancholy half-breed hairy italian, who's got a penchant for singing Janet Jackson in my ear, walk down the corridor of the train station. It's an odd life. . . .

Pulp53

So Doobe and I end up saying good-bye at Heathrow Airport.

"When do ya think yu'll come back to America?"

"I don't know . . . Maybe soon . . . My grandfather's real sick . . . And I'm thinkin' about goin' back to school . . . What are you gonna do, Jimi?"

"I guess it's back to the races for me . . . I don't think I've been gone long enough to clear my debts or anything . . . What is it . . . 7 years, right?"

"Jimi . . . You definitely ARE a runner, I'll say that."

"I'm a dancer." We laugh and hug. I know we won't see each other for a long time. Something passed between us in Paris, with Jane, and me leaving, not wanting to share their laughter and tears. Maybe the thing that brought us together, Ray, is now the thing that makes us not be able to stay together. We remember, and then we have to forget. We try to forget, so we can go on.

"Jimi . . . I'm just glad you made it over . . . You're always welcome on my couch, buddy."

I give him a last squeeze and I walk up the runway to the plane. I think he meant it . . . That I'd always be welcome on his couch . . . But I know it's over. Whatever IT is, I know IT'S gone. I can't be showing up on their couches anymore—all these people I used to know, went to school with, hung out with. My tour of yesterday is over. I've milked it out: boarding school, college, the whole east coast schoolboy party circuit is way old. I gotta blame it on that, on them. There aren't too many other things I can point the finger at. The show's over, and I'm still taking bows like there's a full house in front of me.

Pulp54

"Jimi . . . Why didn't we make love last night?" she says, rolling over, up and outta bed, deftly avoiding my sleepy lunge. "Oh shit . . . I'm already late for class."

Back in Hell and it's colder than ever. Two months of enlightened self-annihilation hadn't meant shit. Hostage to HER emotions and MY pain-lust. She's pacing the room in a frenzy, throwing dirty panties, trying to unearth a cigarette, and I'm wondering what's happened. As IF it could change. As IF ME going away was going to change her, or it, or this, or me. TV shows go on hiatus and so does bad love . . . And they both always pick up right where they left off.

"I don't know, Linds . . . I think it's HARD for two people to fuck when ONE of'm is running circles around the room . . . A question of physics really." What am I supposed to do? Act as puzzled as she is? She's not puzzled at all. She just hates me and doesn't realize it. I see it, though . . . I think I even feel it myself.

"Do you always have to use the word FUCK . . . You're really a pig!"

"Lindsey, of all the ridiculous things I STILL do . . . Saying that you and I make LOVE is not one of them."

She stops moving and stares at me with a set of eyes that only Charlie Manson would call sexy. Pure hate. I'm held down by the gaze as if each eye is a spike holding me, running through me, pinning me to the mattress, piercing my lungs and making me real scared. That's it . . . REAL SCARED!

"You're just so morbid!" and spins out into the hallway.

Spikes removed, I claw my way to the end of the bed with a jaundiced eye on the bathroom.

Standing in the bathroom, listening to the spray hit, and jerking my way through a full-on pee-shiver, I see the back of her head storm through the room and bound back out, accompanied by a series of disgusted groans. It's painful to look at the bitch from any angle. It's funny. It's actually just funny. I can't help but laugh . . . The emotions . . . The time . . . Even Europe all seems like such a waste because I did it for her. Jimi Banks became an expatriate because he was lovesick for a girl who just really isn't happy when he's around. The piss hitting the bowl, splashing back up in my hand. Always dirty, always getting dirty. Puke on my face . . . Piss on my hands . . . Shit on my nose. It's all so beautiful . . . And it's just so filthy. I could hope all I want, that some cosmic eclipse would erase every mishap, every misword, every misfuck, but I just don't think it matters anymore. The hate had taken on a life of its own. When our eyes meet, puppets come up from out of our psyches and spit on each other. FUCK IT . . . SHE'S SUCH AN ASSHOLE ANYWAYS . . . WHERE DID OUR LOVE GO? . . . BACK WHERE IT CAME FROM . . . THANK FUCKING GOD . . . IT DOESN'T MATTER . . . I'M AN ASSHOLE TOO . . . IT DOESN'T MATTER WHO'S WHO OR WHAT'S WHAT . . . I mean . . . There's no doubt I'm a selfish drunken bum fag coward liar and whatever else fits. But at least I'm not stringing this shitty thing along and pretending I don't see it. I see. I see. And now I'm fucking out of here.

I walk out of the bathroom and there she is, buzzing around the living room all pissed off. I start to laugh out loud.

"You're happy I missed my class, aren't you, Jimi?"

"I wish it were that painless . . . This laughter's taken months, miles, and so many dollars to muster."

"What?"

"I shoulda laughed this laugh back in July . . . It's been rotting inside of me and choking me because I've been afraid to let it out."

"Oh now, we're gonna have THIS talk again . . . !"

"I was standing in the bathroom looking at every angle, every little wall, every brush, every bottle, every THING in there, and all I saw was us, and none of it was any good . . . I hate every bit of it . . . Linds, I'm goin' back to the island . . . We're through . . . Not that that's any BIG news to you . . . I'm just saying it out loud for my OWN good . . . I gotta get outta here."

"OK . . . Well . . . You know," she says, stopping, ". . . Call me or maybe I'll call you . . . I mean someday . . . I wanna know what you're up to . . . You know. . . ."

The moment. The moment when it's finally been said and a small piece of truth creeps back in. The faces relax, and the eyes soften, and I see again. Lindsey becomes a human again. No longer a goddess or a monster . . . Just the girl I fell in love with. I run my fingers through her hair and down the side of her face. The anger subsides for the first time in months.

"I do . . . I gotta go, Linds."

"I know."

"I don't really want to though."

"Something's gotta change . . . This is hell on both of us, Jimi."

"I'm afraid to leave you."

"I think it'd be better."

Looking at her face as I stroke her hair. Talking to her again. No shadowboxing, just words. It doesn't matter what the words mean when they're put together. It's just nice to hear them again. Hoping I can make something from nothing, wishing.

"Can we make LOVE one more time, Linds?" Hating that I said it, but feeling a need to say it. Trying to find some last piece. ". . . And then I gotta go . . . I gotta leave here . . . This place makes me sad anymore . . . I'm fucked up about it . . . Can we do that?"

"Ah . . . Yeah . . . OK . . . I've already missed my class anyways." And gets back in bed.

I get in next to her and start to give her kisses. Our tongues occasionally brush past one another. Lindsey's got her sweater on and I'm naked. I'm at the Final Chapter and she's missing her lecture. IT'S HORRIBLE. AND IT'S PERFECT. I kiss her down her bare thighs until I get to the inside of her. I lick and kiss the folds. I take each lip into my mouth and suck on it. Pulling her apart . . . Thinking of other things . . . Thinking of other times . . . Trying to be tender . . . Her body feels tense and cold . . . But there's warmth inside of her . . . I peek up at her face . . . The eyes are closed . . . She's left me . . . I hate myself for trying to make this something new again. I should've just kissed her and left, but that little piece of me still hopes. The HUMAN in me. Going back to what once was . . . Remembering the laughter . . . Remembering the good . . . Thinking just maybe . . . She begins rubbing herself while I rock inside . . . It lasts a couple of minutes and then we come. The desperation rolling down my body in frozen beads. I give her a kiss.

"Is there anything left here? Anything at all?"

"No, Jimi . . . You were right before."

I get up and put my clothes on. It's still early in the morning. Early enough for me to get out to the island without ever having to deal with any REAL world.

Lindsey follows me through the apartment to the front door. I turn around as my hand twists the knob. I wanna cry but I feel like I'll pass out or something weird if I let it all loose. Lindsey looks serene, calm. I can tell by the stillness that THIS is how it should really be. The birds outside. I hear them. The sun. I feel it. Nature tells me. I remember the first time I saw her, sitting on the Navigator porch in her waitress outfit, laughing and drinking with her friends. I take her hands in mine. They're warm.

"You know . . . I'll never forget the first time I saw you . . . I thought you were the most beautiful girl to've ever come out to the island . . . Here it is . . . The summer's over . . . You and I lived together . . . And now, we're saying good-bye . . . It was beautiful, wasn't it? . . . I mean I remember it all being so good when it was happening. . . ."

"Jimi . . ." she says, and squeezes my hand just tight enough for me to feel her one last time. ". . . It was a nice summer . . ." and lets go of my hand and turns away. ". . . It really was."

I walk down the stairs and out of the building. A stray cat runs in front of me. The air is crisp, the sun is climbing. There's no wind. Cars hurry past me on the street. I hoist my bag over my shoulder, straightening my jacket under the strap, looking for a train or a bus or anything to leave on. All the other people seem to be walking down the hill, so I turn right and start after them. I look over my shoulder up at her window, trying to catch one last glimpse . . . Maybe just a shadow, anything, a last tiny piece . . . And then I leave. . . .

Pulp55

Standing out on a narrow stretch of beach with high grass to my right, watching the ocean roll in when I think of it, drinking buck-fifty bottles of red wine, reliving the joys, and then tasting the bitter. In and out . . . Over and over . . . Synchronicity . . . A gulp of juice . . . A picnic on the beach . . . The last time I saw her . . . A telephone I can't pick up . . . The waves roll in and take it back out, only to wash it back in again. How many times can I tell her I'm sorry and how many times will I not accept the apology? . . . A shell is forming around me . . . A beard on my jaw . . . A smile on my mouth . . . A joke on my tongue . . . I've retreated . . . The sand sparkles and shines in front of me . . . A strip of light across my vision . . . I lay in wait under the shadow of a bottle I hold over my head . . . I've been to this place before . . . But I always lied and told myself I had somewhere else to go . . . The sea is my movie . . . Thinking something must happen . . . And knowing it won't come from me . . . Waiting. . . .

Pulp56

The island clears out with the weather. LATE FALL. Work's hard to find. Islanders hold on to their work. If there are only two houses to paint, then they do it alone and stretch it out over the winter. If they don't know me, they don't care. If they do know me, they won't hire me. It's a small place and a reputation can ruin. My rep is "he's an OK guy to get drunk with, but don't hire him for anything." They buy me a drink, hand me a couple bucks, and casually tell me to shut up. As long as I get the drink . . . I DO shut up. It goes like that for weeks. A couch here, a buck there, a free meal—just enough to stay conscious. Finally, Joe Duffy takes me on as his mate and I become a lobsterman.

Galloping across the water on the roof of his 31-foot rig with R.E.M. cranking, smoking a joint while Joe steers through the roof with a broomstick. We rise up and then drop in with each swell. This ain't the Love Boat but it sure beats raking leaves for a ham sandwich and a six-pack—my last gig. We're a piece of driftwood out here, ducking and jiving like a scared flyweight. I'm as small as I suspected. NOTHING. The depressing french guys are right.

We work all day, sometimes I clear a C-note. Sometimes I make twenty. Either way, Joe buys me two poached with hash every morning, and a bucket of beers every night. Fuck the car payments, they can have it back if they want it.

Being out on the water gets confusing. Nothing to do but think, and yet, one loose rope catches an ankle and it's over. It's about Lindsey. It's about money. It's about Ray. It's about an empty trap landing in front of me. I open the trap, tear the fish in half, jam it into the bait box, close the trap and throw the trap off the back of the moving boat. The traps are strung 7 or 8 together, so there's no time to stop. Joe's already throwing the next trap back at me. A string of traps will snap your leg like it's a dry twig, pulling you into the water before you even know it. The bait fish sit rotting in the sun in 100-gallon drums until I open them every morning with a stomach full of last night's booze. When I tear them in half, the spines snap and pierce my heavy rubber gloves, so my hands are always infected and bleeding.

A couple of times a day, Joe pulls up a trap and there's a sea eel caught inside. Joe dumps it out in the boat and either stomps on its head, or lets it swim around on the floor. "You little raunchy cunts! How do ya like me now? How do ya like me now with a squashed head!" All the time yelling, "Ahoy matey" or just howling in general. I don't like the eels at all, alive or dead. They're big . . . 3 . . . 4 . . . 5 feet long and thick like fire hoses.

Mean, with hate in their eyes and mouths. All they want to do is get back in the cold dark ocean and get on with their lives. But they can't. They're either too retarded from Joe's boot to the skull, or they haven't found the little drain hole yet. Sometimes, they're too fat for the drain hole and they have to wait for the next big wave to come over the side and set them free. They writhe between my legs and scowl at me as I tear rotting vile fish in half. My stomach jumps like a volcano on angel dust. Back and forth between my legs, rubbing on my boots, waiting for me to lean too far over, waiting for me to be next to them. Joe could care less, they don't bother him. They bother me though . . . They know they can get to me.

Joe's from Boston. We tended bar together over the summer. I think he got sick of hearing me bitch back at the bar. I always thought he hated me, so one day I mustered all my courage and told him to FUCK OFF . . . Then he started to love me. The best thing about Joe, other than his girlfriend, who I desperately want to fuck, is a long J-shaped scar that he has down the line of his jaw, on the left side of his face. I don't know how he got it. It's so big that I'm afraid to ask. It had to be something horrendous, and I've got an honest respect for Joe's insanity, especially now that he's got MY life in his hands every day. When we're out on the water, I don't ask him about his girl, or his big scar, I just tear the fish.

"Joe . . . Don't you ever get lonely out here?"

"No, Jimi me boy . . . But I do get horny sometimes."

Oh yeah, that's the other thing. Joe thinks he's like Ahab or something, with the "Ahoy" and the "me boy" stuff . . . Who knows?

"How's that bitty, Lindsey . . . Do ya ever hear from her or anything?"

"Not really . . . I . . . We . . . Broke that thing off when I got back from London."

"That's a shame, matey . . . She had such lovely BUOYS . . . Wasn't a real smart girl though. . . ."

I'd never thought about whether or not Lindsey was smart. I don't know WHAT I thought about her as a person. All I ever saw was my little image, just part of some movie I'm trapped in. With the eels, and the water stinging the cuts in my hand, and the stomach churning, that's where Lindsey is, in my stomach, all just part of what's making me sick—some mix of nausea and emptiness.

". . . Are ya gonna see her again or what?"

"I hope not."

"Ya mean that?"

"I don't know . . . Do I?"

"Look, I don't wanna be one to pry . . . But I AM feeding your drunken ass these days . . . And I gotta tell you that you're dying . . . Maybe it's not her . . . Maybe I'm all wrong . . . Maybe I'm just a BIG ASSHOLE . . . I mean, I know I'm THAT anyways . . . But you better figure out whatever it is and get the fuck on with it. . . ."

"I don't know, I mean . . . We said good-bye and I

think we BOTH knew that it was definitely over . . . We haven't spoken since." Right then, a swell hits the boat and water rushes over the side. There's action on the boat as trapped eels heave themselves about, trying to get back into the sea. I get thrown over, across the boat, and Joe grabs me. There's a second where our eyes meet . . . This guy . . . Helping me, trying to keep me up and me wavering . . . Too weak to stand on my own . . . Joe looking at me like he doesn't trust me.

"Thanks man!" I say, spitting out a mouthful of ocean.

"You gotta see those comin' . . . I told you to watch the fuckin' swells . . . They come in sets . . . You'da been dead in 45 seconds if you went in that water . . . Yur like a fuckin' zombie!"

The boat settles back down and I look over the side. A string of traps trails under the hull of the boat, like tiny shadowy coffins on a leash.

"That water's cold isn't it?"

"Fuckin' right it's cold . . . Lemme tell ya somethin', me boy . . . What you need is some fresh pussy . . . The only way to forget the old stuff is to kill it with somethin' better . . ." he says as he throws an empty cage at my head. ". . . Sometimes I fuck a broad just to keep some distance between me and the old lady . . . Nothin' like some side pussy to keep the steady pussy in line . . . But that isn't what you need . . ." Another trap comes sailing. ". . . You need somethin' to make you forget . . . You're losin' it . . . And out here on the water, it ain't safe for either of us, if you're all lovesick . . ." Another trap lands at my feet, as I jam a bloody shred of a fish into the trap in front of me.

"Yeah, you're probably right . . ." I say as I toss the cage over the back and open the next.

"PROBABLY . . . I AM RIGHT . . . Some fresh pussy'll help heal the wound . . . But I'm tellin' ya, in two weeks, I won't need you anymore out here, and the island'll be empty . . . Nothin' but scary clam-head pussy out here in the winter . . . With the sun goes the fine cunt!"

"So whatta ya think I oughta do?"

"Get some money from somebody and GET THE FUCK OUTTA HERE!"

PuIp57

Small problems have a way of growing up into big problems. Money's that kinda thing. Time's just the opposite. One minute, I got money in my hand and life's beautiful, and the next thing I know, time's up, and I need money. The days get shorter and the bar tabs get longer and the lobsters learn to hide better and I gotta start makin' calls. It's a sensitive thing. You gotta call a person up, make them feel special, ask about their life, be happy, tighten the bond. Everybody's got a little extra money to lend, it's just a matter of becoming worthy of the deed. It's a whole game, a mind-set. I knew it was inevitable. Time and money. Time and money. Time to find the money.

I make a few preliminary calls to some old stand-bys, just to get a feel for the terrain: old room-mates, uncles, sisters. There's always mom and dad, but that's a whole other can of worms. The trick IS to get money from people you don't really have to deal with all that much. I try to borrow a couple hundred from the parents, and who knows what kind of strings might be attached. I might have to make a promise that entails a haircut or something. I mean, the thought HAS crossed my mind, but as a rule, MOM AND DAD ARE THE LAST RESORT. Every day I roam the streets and the bars, saying my hellos, bumming shots, and flip-ping through the Rolodex of my mind. A call here, a message there, NO LUCK. One day, as I sit at the end of the bar at D. Ryan's, trying to turn a fiver into a blackout, BINGO! Who is it . . . Who is it that feels responsible for my well being? Who is it that's gotta deep paternal vibe for me . . . Maybe even loves me? BINGO . . . The Godfather!

Tony Unsel, a.k.a. Antonio Unsellino. YES . . . The italian bloodlines, so slyly hidden behind names like Banks and Unsel, produce things like godfathers. Tony owns a big plumbing business in Cleveland. I drink for another week just waiting to make the call. CHEAP METHOD ACTING. The more dire my situation becomes, the better I'll be. My sanity on a fine line, my well-being long gone. I'm obsessed with the money. Getting the money, finding the money, money's the answer. Money'll get me through this, it's all about money. Sweat on my palms, greasy hair brushed from outta my face, I sit in bathrooms, looking into mirrors after I piss, rehearsing for the moment, THE BIG CALL. I haven't talked to Uncle Tony in years. Our only communication is a C-note in my mailbox every Christmas. Enough for me to ONLY say the best things about my Uncle Tony. Hands trembling as I dial, butterflies in the stomach, urine stinging only the shaft of my limp penis. It would be hard to feel like less of a man. The phone rings twice before the secretary answers.

"Hi, yeah . . . Is Mr. Unsel in? This is Jimi Banks, his godson." I give her the full family deal because I know it carries a lot of weight around the office. It's the heavy italian trip with all the guilt and pathos trimmings. When I was little, I thought Tony was the richest guy in the world. Every visit to his house came complete with a no-holds-barred run to Children's Palace. The answer to all my HOT WHEEL prayers. The secretary asks me if I can hold. I say "yes."

Waiting is no good, the fog begins to clear and I start to feel stupid. What am I doing? I haven't spoken to this guy in years. I become aware of my hand holding the phone . . . The wind in my face, whipping around the corner of the phone booth . . . My sweaty sore toes wriggling in my wet boots . . . And the tremble of my torso . . . The stomach tightening, trying to stop the shaking . . . Am I cold? . . . Or am I just scared? . . . The waiting . . . It's too long . . . I don't wanna think like this . . . All last week's prep lost in this waiting . . . I'm a wreck . . . I'm a loser . . . I don't even know this fucking guy . . . Who is he . . . Who am I . . . How do we even know each other . . . Maybe he doesn't even know me . . . I'm drowning . . . I'm dying . . . I don't wanna be this aware . . . He's going through a bad divorce . . . I only hope the pain has made him more desperate to be good to OTHER members of the family . . . Help the old godson out . . . Right a few wrongs somewhere else in the world . . . I'll just ask him for 400, it sounds better than 500 . . . NO . . . I'll tell him I need work . . . Act like I wanna be a man, solve my own problems . . . Things are slow for him . . . He won't wanna hassle with the unions, he'll offer me cash . . . I'll be on my way to anywhere! The phone clicks.

"Hello?"

"Uncle Tony . . . It's Jimi Banks, how ya doin'?"

"Good, Jimi . . . Where are you?"

"Actually, I'm pretty far away, up north, off Cape Cod . . . We gotta good connection, don't we?" I blurt, trying to make small talk. It's tough to put a make on Tony's mood; between him being at the office and my angst-storm, I'm scrambling.

"So what's up, Jimi?"

"Well, Unc . . . " stressing the UNC, emphasizing the family bond. "Things're actually kinda tough right now . . . And I was wondering if maybe I couldn't drop down there and hook into a few quick weeks of work with you?" I'd done a summer with the Uncle when I was 15. "I gotta make some car payments in a hurry and I'm getting evicted from my place. It gets real slow up here after the tourists leave . . . I was hoping maybe I could come and carry some pipe for you . . . Make some money to get out to L.A. with." It seemed to make so much sense when I was drunk at the bar, but now it really sounded weak! I'm losing! None of this makes sense. I've lost faith in my lie. They don't believe it if YOU don't!

"I wish I could say 'yes,' Jimi, but I don't have enough work to keep my own boys busy. You're a little too old to sneak by the unions . . . They'd think you're a SCAB . . . It wouldn't be good, even if I COULD do it."

Like a prank call I can't hang up on. Pacing around the booth on a leash with a target on my back.

"Oh yeah . . . Things are that slow, huh?"

"Things are REAL slow."

No one's taking anyone's lead. It's a stalemate and I'm drowning in the process. No familiar tones, this is NOT the same guy who used to shower me in G.I. Joes and I'm not that funny little kid . . . Or maybe, that's exactly what I am? I go for broke.

"Unc, maybe we could talk about a little loan

then? Sort of a belated graduation present, you know I graduated from college, didn't you? I'm in a real bind up here! I don't have enough money to get my car off the island! I'm trapped . . . I wouldn't be calling you like this, if I didn't have to!"

A silence ensues, and from where I'm standing, it can't be TOO GOOD. I've done everything but beg. There's no control, it became something I didn't want it to become. I've lost my form, I have no form, no ground to stand on. This talk, this conversation, became a plea to someone, to anyone, to everyone.

"You know, it's funny, Jimi, I haven't heard from you in five or six years. I haven't SEEN you since high school and you worked for me that one summer . . . I send you money every year at the holidays without so much as a single thank-you note, not even a phone call . . . And now, you interrupt me in the middle of my work day, from out of nowhere, and you ask me for money . . . What did YOU think I was going to say? I mean, Christ, you coulda called me once last month or something, but no, outta nowhere you call. . . ."

"Look, Unc . . . I know it's kinda weird," I say, grasping. "I had some work I thought was coming up and it fell through . . . I don't know where else to go. I can't call my dad. I don't wanna look like a failure in his eyes . . . You were the only person I could think of."

"I'll tell you what," he says, finally, "let me make some calls . . . See if anyone around here has anything. Call me back next week, before Wednesday, because I'm going away."

"So you'll see if anyone's got a little work for me?"

"Yeah . . . Lemme see what's out there."

"Well, if there isn't any out there, Unc . . . Then maybe we could talk about a little loan?"

"Yea, we'll talk then. Look, I gotta go now, Jimi, so call me," and CLICK.

To say that I feel like the lowest worm right now would be to speak with a certain degree of confidence. The clarity of the moment, THINKING I'm a slick petty con man, and SEEING that I'm really just a BEGGAR. Just a pleading, apologizing, stroking little beggar with no respect or balls.

I never DO make that second phone call to Uncle Tony. There isn't a glass of whiskey in this world strong enough to give me the guts to make that one. I never even thought about sending the guy a lousy thank-you note? What a mistake. No form, no form at all.

Pulp 58

The days melt into weeks, the weeks into a slow-motion blur. Wake up every morning with the brain pumping ugly thoughts and it never stops. Will it be bourbon? Or will I start off with a draft to lube it up? Maybe some weed? Anything'll do, nothing'll matter. Hiding out on a shut-down island, calling in old debts from my bartending days, and trying to make new ones wherever I can. Torn dirty khakis stick to the insides of my legs. A faded blue sweatshirt and a grey felt hat that I stole from Helms. I hang out. Waiting. I don't make phone calls, I just show up places. Looking to kill a few months with a TV remote in one hand and a bottle in the other, alone. No work left. Looking for that odd twenty-spot, wondering who to ask. The number's getting harder and harder to come up with. Good luck, I got good luck in a bad way. The sun shines, the rain falls and life passes by, spiralling down like the last piece of shit in a toilet bowl. I think about the past and I think about that next twenty. No point looking beyond that, there's just another twenty waiting to be found, right behind it. My old bar throws me free drinks until the paying folks show up, then I gotta get lost. I stumble back to the kitchen at that point, and see the head cook, Paul. I used to feed'em good scotch back in the days when I could, and I don't let'em forget.

"Paulie . . . Buddy . . . How's about a little sangwitch to fill my stomach with . . . I'm fuckin' hungry!"

"No Jimi . . . I'm sorry pal . . . Enough's enough."

The warmth of the kitchen starts my body shaking. I didn't realize how cold it is. My hands're swollen, the air outside, grey and heavy, pushing in through the window. It's too small, it's all too small in here.

"Come on, Paulie . . . You wouldn't let Jimi starve, would you?"

"I'm not letting YOU do anything . . . YOU BUM . . . Why don't you get a fuckin' job!"

"I would get a job, but there aren't any left out here!"

"Well then . . . Why don't you take a fuckin' hint and leave . . . Whatta you, retired?"

The window's pushing in, the cold air, the grey, heaviness, everything feels so heavy, my chest, my hands all swollen, my feet all wet, my head all fucked up, I gotta leave this island, the same song day in and day out . . . My stomach's burning . . . Acid washing around inside . . . "Get a job asshole," the cook next to him says, and starts to laugh . . . I hear it . . . I see those big teeth laughing . . . Moving up and down . . . I hear them clapping together . . . Come on man, I'm gonna leave this island, just a bite of something . . . Get a life, hahaha . . . I'm fuckin' trying, man . . . Hands purple and swollen . . . You're tryin', well it isn't working out, hahaha . . . What about all those good scotches I gave you . . . Fuck 'em, hahaha . . . Just a little something, I reach with the hands, anything . . . Here you go, asshole, take this and chew on it . . . Carrots start to fly at me, bouncing off my face, stinging me. I cover my face and duck down, I begin picking up the carrot ends and chewing them. They're filthy, sand, mud, rocks, dirt, in my mouth, grinding, my hands aching, nails scratching on the cold tile, wishing, wishing I was anywhere, the air all cold, the feet in front of me, no more aces up my sleeve, laughter, laughing at me again, dirt in my mouth, chewing, acid in my stomach, everyone hates me, nobody likes me anymore. My fingers stretch out for another carrot, dirt in my mouth, crunching, they hate me, a tree in my mind, dirt in my mouth. I wanna be free, I wanna, I wanna be, purple fingers reach, a tree, a noose, what do I do, swallowing, chewing, a body in a tree, everyone laughing at me, throwing food at me, hating me, fuck, fuck, fuck, he's hanging in a noose, dirt in my mouth, Ray's hanging in a tree, dirt in my mouth, reaching out to touch, laughter and sneering, me unable to be anywhere else, scratching for food, for carrots, for dirt, clawing, carrots come stinging with laughter, beyond shame, hitting off my head, off my face, unable to hide inside, can't tell them to stop, it's not them, it's me, it's not them, it's me, it's not them, it's me . . . I . . . Am him, he is me, I am . . . A ray. I am ray. I am Ray, I hang from the tree . . . EPIPHANY . . . I look up through my hands and see all the little movies of my life running through the webs of my fingers. Carrots fly through my weak shield. A child. I was once a happy little boy. All I tried to be, escape. Run, run, run, run over the waterfall I tried to run from. Dirty carrot heels stinging my face. Stop time. Hiding deep in my breathing corpse, watching the final scene. Helpless. Can't leave my chair. Can't be anywhere but here, in me. Trapped, being him, knowing him. My life, an answer to a riddle, "Whatever happened to . . . ? . . . Well lemme tell ya, let me show ya, let me BE him!" A ray of light, of hope, of death, of truth. Slow motion, through fingers, carrot ends soar like shovels of dirt on top of me, our small tragedy, my little tail. A shared moment, defenseless, watching in silence while fate pelts my face over and over, stinging and laughing. Can't stop it, don't want to. Seeing who I never grew up to be. Down on knees, hands fallen at my sides. No more movies, no more cool songs, just me. Tears carving cold ruts in my face. Dirty carrots raining on me. Unable to fight, to care. No more tricks, just truth. Over and over. Laughter and pity. A radio blares on through the brittle grey air. WINTER. The loneliness of finally knowing, of finally seeing. No whistle loud enough to keep me company. Not wanting to be him, but relieved that I finally am . . . Seeing. Alone. Being. I am Ray . . . Shame . . . Tears . . . Surrender . . . Silence. . . .

Pulp59

I'm standing at the mouth of the Russian River where it opens out into the Pacific and I'm so far away from all that. There are about thirty seals lounging on the beach just beyond the tide. It's cold. It's fall. I just quit my job and left L.A. STILL RUNNING. 257 days. Nothing but blood running through my veins. The seals could care less, but I do. Somebody told me about the seals and I got to thinking that I needed to see it with my own eyes. Just laying there, happy. Every once in awhile they stretch and roll around a little bit, just like my cats. I drove 500 miles to see these seals. Really see them, see something other than me. Drove 500 miles to see something beautiful. They look like big wet dogs. I'm about 3 feet away from them. Maybe I'll move here one day. I start thinking about Doobe and London. I think about Paris. 500 miles to see something. Beauty feeds me. I wonder what Harry did when he found those socks? I hope he laughed. I laugh now, I let out a nice big laugh. Happy to laugh, heals me. I think about Lindsey . . . And yeah, I think about Ray. We both died. I am alive. Maybe I'll always think about Ray. Hope I always remember. All those people and all those places and I'm wondering if I should pet these seals. 257 days. Nothing but blood running through my veins. NO POISON. Trying to live, sick of not dying, sick of quitting. I think about Diane and I wonder if seals bite? Whatever happened to so many people? I think about Rosie and I wonder if she ever found love? No one writes . . . No one ever writes anymore . . . We all lose touch . . . Maybe I should call someone? The water comes in and the seals all roll around a little. In and out, in and out, rolling around. I see one yawn. He's got big white fangs and long black whiskers. Oh yeah, Doobe's in South America. I'd like to call Lindsey, I think she's in Chicago now. I'm standing in between all these roly seals and I'm still pretty lost . . . But I'm alive. I'll probably go back to L.A. . . . I never thought I wanted any of it to end . . . 257 days . . . Looking for another beginning . . . Looking for a new place to start. . . .

Los Angeles, CA 1993

Arty Nelson, born Pittsburgh, PA, 1965. Suburbia. Kent School. Colgate University. Work appeared in *Caffeine*, *bikini*, *Tales of the Heart*. Lives in L.A.